The Wave Traveller

Also by P. R. Morrison

The Wind Tamer

The Wave Traveller

P. R. Morrison

BLOOMSBURY

472040

With thanks to Sarah Odedina,
Georgia Murray and Isabel Ford, who
see beyond the horizon.

First published in Great Britain in 2007 by Bloomsbury Publishing Plc
36 Soho Square, London, W1D 3QY

A CIP catalogue record of this book is available from the British Library

ISBN 978 0 7475 8781 1

All papers used by Bloomsbury Publishing are natural, recyclable products made
from wood grown in well-managed forests. The manufacturing processes conform
to the environmental regulations of the country of origin.

Typeset by Dorchester Typesetting Group Ltd
Printed in Great Britain by Clays Ltd, St Ives Plc

1 3 5 7 9 10 8 6 4 2

www.bloomsbury.com

This book is dedicated to Cameron,
Jemma, Jamie and Kirsten

Prologue

The Glimpers had been asleep for a hundred years, deep beneath the North Sea, where neither sunlight nor moonlight could disturb their rest. Whales, sharks and strange fish with dead eyes drifted above their crusted backs, and the sunken debris of warships lay close to where they lay but still they slept, cocooned in layers of sand and silt. Perhaps they would have slept another hundred years, but change was on the way.

A bright full moon rose up in the February sky, bringing with it high tides and dangerous undercurrents, but the effect of this turbulence was felt most strongly on the seabed, far from human eyes. The watery storm swept the sand from the Glimpers' shells and they emerged from their resting place: thousands upon thousands, row upon row. Some resembled black oval stones the size of a man's hand, others were as large as a rowing boat. Slowly they opened their crab-like eyes, and the ocean bed appeared to move as each one raised itself upon eight unsteady legs and stood to attention.

As the sand resettled on the ocean floor, a single Glimper emerged out of their midst holding a green pebble in its claw. This was the signal the army had been waiting for. A century had passed since the sea had last called them to battle, but now the time had come again, and with their pincers held high the Glimpers began the long and dangerous march north towards the battlegrounds of Westervoe.

FOUR WEEKS LATER

Chapter One

The first time Archie Stringweed heard the sound of a distant marching army, he was scrambling over a rocky headland where strong tides meet and armies of soldiers do not march.

He spun round, expecting to see an advancing legion, but all he saw was a single herring gull surfing the breeze, and his parents, who were gazing intently into a rock pool. Beyond them lay empty white sand stretching far into the distance. Yet still the sound of marching continued.

Archie decided it was the echo of breaking waves on the other side of the headland, for what other explanation could there be? But one week later he heard that same marching sound again.

It was a quiet Sunday morning down at Westervoe harbour and he was fishing with his friends, George and Sid. An hour had passed without a single bite and to add to the boys' disappointment the tide had turned.

Archie leaned over the harbour railings and stared down through the clear water to the seabed. An empty lemonade bottle was sticking up out of the silt close to a black shoe that had no lace, and a large clump of seaweed was floating gently towards the opposite pier, but there was not one single fish to be seen.

Archie tried to remain hopeful. 'Maybe we should try deeper water.'

But neither Sid nor George were interested. In fact the only response came from a herring gull now circling overhead. It was a rather battered-looking gull with an unusual line of black feathers beneath one wing, and it gave a long echoing cry as Archie walked the length of the harbour towards a slipway that took him down to the water's edge.

The first thing he glimpsed when he looked on to the sea was his reflection, a dark, gently moving outline of himself, and he raised his hand to flatten the persistent tuft of hair sticking out above his right ear. Then he lay down on his stomach and leaned over the edge until his nose was almost touching the water and focused on what lay beneath. There were no fish to be seen, but to his surprise two small perfectly round black eyes were peering up at him out of the seaweed-encrusted wall. The eyes were glassy and strangely hypnotic, and as he leaned closer to determine what kind of creature they belonged to, another set of eyes emerged out of the seaweed and then another and another until there were hundreds of pairs of eyes all staring up at him – patiently, as if waiting for a signal.

Archie found he couldn't resist looking into these eyes. He could hear strange, high-pitched wailing, too, and as he listened he felt his mind begin to empty. All he could think of was how inviting the water looked; that it resembled a big soft watery pillow waiting to be lain upon. The more this thought filled his head, the more he relaxed, and as his eyes began to close he was aware of a shadow moving over the sea towards him. A cold shiver ran through his body, a faraway voice called out his name and then his head slipped beneath the surface and everything went black.

Chapter Two

Archie tried opening his eyes, but couldn't. He tried lifting his head out of the cold water, but couldn't. He found himself completely paralysed and unable to resist the snake-like sensation creeping around the back of his neck. But he liked the silence.

A loud screech pierced his ear and he was aware of rushing water . . . cold air . . . voices shouting . . . and he opened his eyes into daylight. His face was hovering above the sea's surface and his scalp ached from someone holding his hair by the roots.

Salt water was running down his cheeks and pouring out of his nostrils and mouth. He blinked and remembered to breathe as he was pulled up into a sitting position.

'What were you trying to do?' George was asking. 'Drown yourself?'

Archie shook his head and droplets of water shot out from his face and hair. He gasped for air and then came the words. 'Did you see them?'

'Dead bodies?' said Sid, who always feared the worst.

'Eyes!' said Archie. He spat out salt water. 'Hundreds of them.'

Sid pulled a grey crumpled handkerchief out of his trouser pocket. It appeared to have been glued together by something unspeakable. He held it towards Archie, who declined the offer, preferring to use his fingers to squeeze the dripping water from his fringe.

George meantime was looking down into the sea. 'I can't see any eyes.'

Sid took a look too. 'Me neither.'

Archie crawled to the water's edge and stared down at an eye-free wall. 'But they *were* there,' he insisted, 'hundreds of them.'

George picked up his fishing rod. 'Probably just seaweed,' he decided. 'I'm hungry. Let's get something to eat? Who's coming?'

Sid was quick to volunteer, but with no money to spend he turned to Archie, who could be relied upon to share. 'Are you coming?' he asked.

Archie nodded, intending to follow them back up the slipway, but a movement beneath the water distracted him. To his left and to his right, hundreds of pairs of eyes were once more emerging out of the seaweed to resume their staring position. He was aware of the high-pitched wailing too, and that sleepy hypnotic sensation creeping up on him again. Archie tried calling out to Sid and George but his voice was barely a whisper. It was then he heard for the second time an army on the march. It was the same steady rhythm he had heard out at the Point headland one week earlier, only this time the marching was coming from beneath the water, and as he listened he was sure he could hear the distinctive clank of armour.

The glassy eyes staring up at him heard it too and darted back into the seaweed, leaving small whirlpools on the water's surface.

The wailing and the sleepy sensation also disappeared and Archie sat up to find a gull hovering in front of him. It was beating its wings wildly and when it gave a warning squawk Archie scuttled away from the water's edge. The bird then turned and flew to the top of the slipway where Sid and George were waiting, and after another echoing cry it prepared to swoop.

Sid was the first to respond. He covered his head with his arms and, with a shrill panicked scream, began to run, but his quick getaway was hindered by wellie boots two sizes too big. George, in brand new trainers, overtook him, pulling the hood of his jacket up over his head for protection as he ran towards the café at the top of the harbour.

Archie grabbed his fishing rod, scrambled to his feet and began to give chase while keeping his eye on the swooping bird. As the boys neared the café door, the gull suddenly changed course and soared up over the rooftops, taking a direct path up the hill towards a large house near the top: an old house with ivy climbing up the walls, a tall tree out front and a brass name-plaque on the garden gate saying 'Windy Edge'. There it settled on a cracked chimney pot close to a skylight window, and after settling its feathers stretched its neck and took a long inquisitive look into Archie's attic bedroom.

Chapter Three

The Harbour View Café was owned by George's Auntie Maggie. She was only slightly taller than George and on first inspection resembled an oversized poodle. Her dark curly hair framed her face like floppy ears and her black-framed glasses were almost hidden by a heavy fringe. You half expected her to bark.

'What's the hurry?' she asked as first George and then Sid charged through the café door.

George was looking particularly wide-eyed. 'There's a mad gull out there.'

'It attacked us,' Sid confirmed in a shaky voice.

Seconds later Archie ran inside to join them. Not only was he breathless, but his hair was wet.

Maggie suspected the situation might not be as straightforward as she had first thought. She stopped wiping the plastic tabletops, stuck her head out of the door, and after taking a good look around the immediate area delivered her report.

'No swooping gulls out here.'

Her blue nylon overall crackled as she resumed wiping a table, but then a thought occurred to her. 'If you boys are scared, I'm quite happy to walk you along the road.'

George looked deeply offended. 'We're not scared!'

Sid was busily nodding in agreement. 'We just thought a swooping gull was kind of interesting.'

Maggie looked thoughtful. 'I bet that gull was after the fish in your bag.'

Sid shook his head. 'But we haven't caught any fish. Not a single bite.'

Maggie pointed towards his fishing bag. 'You got sandwiches in there?'

'No,' Sid told her and he lifted out the only item the bag contained, a beetroot jar full of squirming worms.

Maggie brought her nose up close to the jar.

'Tell you what,' she said. 'You lads look a bit peckish. Why don't you let me fry the worms up for you in a nice crispy batter with a splash of vinegar?'

Archie, George and Sid were threatening to be sick on the spot when a very loud burp came bouncing over the tables towards them.

They turned to see Slaverin' Joe, Maggie's only customer. He was sitting in his usual seat at the back of the café beneath a large picture of the Canadian Rocky Mountains. He wasn't very tall but he was very wide, partly due to the orange waterproof coat he wore all year. He also had the biggest pair of nostrils Archie had ever seen. Slaverin' Joe swallowed a mouthful of tea, raised his shoulders high, threw back his head and released a series of powerful burps that sounded as if he was shooting golf balls. When he was finished, he placed his arms on the table and his dark eyes looked at them from beneath the peak of his filthy red baseball cap.

'Marauding gulls, you say?'

Archie was the only one brave enough to say, 'Yes.'

Slaverin' Joe's nostrils twitched and he growled. 'Just the one gull, you say?'

Because Joe's eyes were fixed firmly on him, Archie felt obliged to nod.

Joe raised a huge hand and stroked his greying beard. 'My guess is he was going for your eyes.'

Sid looked at Archie and gasped.

Joe set his mug of tea down on the table. 'Eyes are the juiciest part of the body . . . to a bird, that is.' He was trying to pierce a pickled onion with his fork, but he kept missing. 'Seen it with my very own eyes back in the spring of '85. A field full of sheep all wandering around, bumping into one another, eyes picked from their sockets by a flock of marauding gulls. Oh aye, you want to be careful of their beaks.' His fork finally pierced the onion and he waved it at Archie. 'Especially you. One green eye and one blue eye, a delicacy in the gull world.'

The three boys watched him place the onion between his mouth. There followed a loud crunch and juice oozed out from the corners of his mouth and slithered into his beard. Slaverin' Joe licked his lips clean.

'Aye. You'll want to be *very* careful.'

There was a moment or two of complete silence as the boys absorbed his words, and then there came the crash of glass smashing against the tiled floor. Sid stared nervously at the pile of worms squirming around his feet amid the shattered glass.

Maggie took one look at the devastation and sighed. 'Well, I guess there goes lunch.'

Chapter Four

After the worms and glass had been cleared from the floor, Maggie provided the boys with three plastic forks and a single complimentary plate of chips. They sat at a table near to the door, shuffling closer together as Slaverin' Joe strode up to the till to pay his bill. He followed the same ritual every Sunday morning before church. A full fried breakfast at the café, ensuring a waft of pickled-onion scented hymns drifted across the congregation.

The boys waited until he was safely out the door before discussing his comments.

'Do you think he was right about the gulls?' Sid wanted to know as he soaked a chip in vinegar.

George shook his head. 'If it was true, they would have pecked our eyes out before now.' He said this while keeping watch on the sky.

Sid wasn't convinced. 'Slaverin' Joe said the gull wants Archie's one blue and one green eye. He said they're *tastier*.'

The boys gave Archie and his eyes a glance, but he wasn't listening. He was thinking about the wall of eyes down at the slipway. Trying to work out how they could all disappear into the seaweed and then reappear at the same time, as if following a command. He was also thinking about how he'd felt when he'd looked into them: a helpless combination of paralysis and hypnotism that had left him feeling shaky. And then there was the sound of that marching army again, like knights in full armour.

'Did you hear marching, just before the gull attacked?' he asked.

'No,' was the short reply from Sid and George because three bowls of ice-cream had been set down on the table.

'You boys had better eat your lunch when you get back home,' Maggie warned them, 'or I'll be for the high jump.'

There were grateful murmurs of 'Thank you very much' while they compared portions. Sid couldn't believe his good fortune but George was less gracious.

'What? No chocolate sauce?'

Maggie picked up his bowl and George was left looking at the empty space on the table where it had stood.

'Hey?' he complained.

Maggie ignored him, and clutching the bowl in her hand she turned her attention to Archie. 'I see your Uncle Rufus is still living with you. Is he planning on staying in Westervoe for good?'

Archie shrugged his shoulders because his mouth was full of ice-cream.

Maggie asked her next question. 'A little bird told me Rufus is teaching your mum to drive. How's she getting on?'

'OK,' Archie managed to say. 'She knows where the dipstick is now.'

Maggie looked impressed. 'Can't be easy driving that big old Land Rover.' She was keeping a tight grip on George's ice-cream bowl even though he was trying to pull it out of her hands. 'I saw Rufus out at the Point the other afternoon when I was walking my dogs,' she told Archie. 'Thought it was your dad, but then of course he would have been at the bank, and then I realised it was Rufus wearing that funny hat of his, striding along the beach without a care in the world.'

Archie carried on eating his ice-cream as Maggie continued her interrogation. 'So what was Rufus doing out there?'

'Don't know.'

'Can I have my ice-cream, Maggie?' George was pleading.

'If I can have some gratitude,' she said over her

shoulder. Then she turned her attention back to Archie.

'Rufus goes out to the Point a lot these days. Quite a few people have seen him come and go. Odd times of day, too.'

If Maggie was expecting some small snippet of information, she didn't get it. Archie didn't like the suspicious way she was talking about Rufus and he pretended to be too busy scraping clean his ice-cream bowl to answer.

George looked on enviously. 'Can I *please* have my ice-cream, Maggie?'

She put the bowl down and he immediately began spooning the ice-cream into his mouth.

Archie and Sid both finished eating and Sid licked his lips. 'Mmmm , I love pineapple ice-cream.'

'Pineapple?' said Maggie. 'Oh no, that wasn't pineapple.' She winked at them before turning to George, whose mouth was packed to bursting. 'I whisked all those worms up and mixed them with vanilla.'

George looked horrified.

Maggie smiled sweetly. 'Well, no point wasting them.'

Chapter Five

A telephone was ringing in the hall of Windy Edge. The gull that was perched on the roof, trying to dislodge a tile with its beak, raised its head and listened. The ringing went unheard by Archie's father, Jeffrey, who at that very moment was jogging up the hill towards the house. He had only recently taken up jogging, which is why he was gasping and sweating a lot.

Archie's mother, Cecille, was also unaware of the ringing phone because she was having a driving lesson with Rufus. They were outside the house in the Land Rover practising hill starts and the sound of the phone was lost in the whine of the engine.

'Less revs, more clutch!' Rufus was insisting as the car rolled back down the hill. He pulled on the handbrake before they mounted the kerb. 'You're just not concentrating, Cecille.'

The phone continued to ring and the gull, now

sitting on the chimney pot above Archie's window, opened its beak, threw back its head and proceeded to perfectly imitate the ringing phone.

This time Cecille heard it. She turned off the engine while still in gear, jumped out of the Land Rover and almost collided with Jeffrey, who was approaching at a slow jog. He looked in through the open car door at Rufus and gasped, 'Three miles . . . forty-five minutes.'

Cecille was slightly breathless herself by the time she had run up the path, leapt up the steps and dashed through the open door into the hall. So preoccupied was she, it didn't occur to her the phone sounded as loud outside the house as it did inside. She picked up the handset.

'Hello? . . . Yes, this is Cecille Stringweed . . . Yes, it is a lovely day.' She wore a puzzled expression as she looked through the open door. 'The weather? Well, it's a bit overcast . . . No, there's been no rain at all this weekend . . . Well, you would expect high tides around the equinox . . . No, I haven't noticed any mist . . .' She was about to answer yet another question about the weather but then changed her mind. 'Excuse me, but who am I talking to?' Her eyes opened wide at the reply. 'Oh! This *is* unexpected . . .' After a minute or two of polite conversation, she said, 'Yes, I do have a pen to hand.' She began writing on a notepad next to the phone. 'I'll certainly pass on the message,' she confirmed. 'He'll be thrilled.'

She had finished taking down the details and was saying, 'Goodbye and thank you very much!' when Jeffrey staggered into the hallway.

'Who was that?' he gasped as he mopped the sweat from his brow.

Cecille took one look at his bright red face and at his legs that were starting to buckle at the knees. 'I think you'd better sit down for this piece of news.'

Archie could sense the excitement as soon as he walked through the front door of Windy Edge. He could hear his mother laughing in the kitchen and saying, 'It's only a matter of time before you're *Sir* Jeffrey Stringweed.'

Archie stood in the kitchen doorway. No one seemed to notice his damp fringe plastered to his forehead.

Cecille and Jeffrey were standing by the sink sharing a joke about tiaras and talking in ridiculously posh voices. Rufus was sitting at the kitchen table, quietly engrossed in the Sunday papers, oblivious to their enthusiastic musings until Cecille asked, 'Rufus? Long or short?'

He looked up at her. 'What?'

'Do these occasions require a long evening dress or just a day dress?'

He thought about it for a second or two before replying, 'I don't think it'll be that formal.' Then he resumed reading an article about the Kalahari Desert.

'Short then?' she decided.

'What's going on?' Archie asked.

'Oh, nothing much,' said Cecille, suddenly noticing him. 'Grandma Stringweed's got a sore toe, the drains are playing up again and . . . oh yes!' She looked proudly at Jeffrey. 'Your father is going to be guest of honour at an International Curse Exterminator ceremony on Wednesday evening. To be held at their Edinburgh headquarters.'

Jeffrey nodded and gave a playful salute.

Archie felt his heart quicken at the mention of I.C.E. 'Are we all going?'

'You bet,' said Jeffrey. 'It's a Stringweed family occasion.'

A smile spread across Archie's face. 'So why are you guest of honour, Dad?'

There was a moment during which Cecille and Jeffrey looked at each other for an answer.

'I imagine it's to do with Dad helping you to break the Stringweed curse,' Cecille decided. 'The invitation is already in the post so I suppose it will explain all when it arrives.' Satisfied with her reply she considered the question again. 'Odd, though, they should phone on a Sunday. Seemed more interested in the weather than giving me details about the ceremony. Wanted to know how much rain we'd had this week. And any signs of unusually high tides or mists. And did we have any *sandbags . . .*'

There was the scrape of a chair being pushed back and Rufus stood up. 'I have to go out. Can I borrow the Land Rover?'

'Sure thing,' said Jeffrey, who seemed surprised at Rufus's sudden flurry of activity.

'Can you stick it through the car wash?' Cecille asked. 'The wheels are thick with sand again.'

'Will you be coming to the ceremony, Rufus?' Archie asked.

'Of course he's coming,' Jeffrey interrupted. 'As I said, it's a family occasion.'

Rufus patted Archie's shoulder. 'It'll be good for you to meet everyone at I.C.E.'

Archie followed him into the hall and, recalling Maggie's words about seeing Rufus out at the Point, asked, 'Where are you going?'

Rufus picked up the car keys from the hook by the door. 'Got a bit of business to see to. Won't be long.' He looked directly at Archie. 'What happened to your hair?'

Archie flicked the fringe from his brow. The full explanation seemed too complicated at that moment, and anyway he didn't want to detract from finding out where Rufus was going, so he simply said, 'I slipped down at the harbour. Got a little wet.'

Rufus's eyes narrowed. 'Did you swallow any water?'

'No.'

'Sure?'

Archie realised he wasn't very sure. 'Well, I don't think so.'

'Might be a good idea if you don't go fishing for a while. Best wait until after the equinox.'

'Why?'

'Tides are dangerous this time of year.'

Just then, Cecille popped her head round the kitchen door.

'Can you pick up milk, Rufus? Two pints should be enough.' Before Rufus could reply she had returned to the kitchen, though they could still hear her voice. 'Don't take too long. Lunch is almost ready.'

Rufus turned to Archie and lowered his voice. 'Let me know if you start to feel unusual.'

'What do you mean, "unusual"?'

'Anything out of the ordinary.'

Archie didn't like what he was hearing. 'You mean if I feel ill?'

'Not ill. Just unusual.' Rufus gave a reassuring smile. 'Nothing to worry about. Only a precaution.' With that he walked out the door.

Archie ran his tongue around the inside of his mouth. He could still taste the ice-cream, but as he licked his lips he detected a trace of salt. 'Most likely from the chips,' he told himself, but he went up to the bathroom and brushed his teeth twice and then to make doubly sure he rinsed with mouthwash. After splashing his face with water he looked in the mirror for signs of something 'unusual'.

Certainly he had felt unusual over the last few months. He had put it down to having been struck by lightning inside Huigor's tornado when he had broken the Stringweed curse. Occasionally his body tingled as if he had just been through the spin cycle of the washing machine, and his ears buzzed as though someone had crept up behind him and crashed cymbals. And he'd gone a whole week when everything tasted of mothballs.

His mother had taken him to the doctor and couldn't stop blushing as she explained that Archie might have been struck by lightning. The doctor had looked at her incredulously. '*Might* have been?' He quickly dismissed her concerns. 'If Archie had been struck by lightning, Cecille, he'd be smoking at the ears and looking decidedly burnt.'

He gave Archie a thorough examination, which included listening to his heart and his chest, shining a light in his ears, eyes and throat, and getting him to say 'Aaah' three times. After checking his reflexes, the doctor leaned back in his chair and pronounced he could find nothing wrong. 'Sometimes we can put these symptoms down to "growing pains",' he explained, and sent them home with a leaflet detailing the importance of vitamins and minerals for a growing body.

That was December. It was now March, and apart from the occasional nightmare about Huigor and his ghostly voice predicting, 'Where the night and shadows meet, there shall I lie,' all Archie's symptoms had disappeared. He had also discovered one positive side effect of being struck by lightning: he no longer wheezed when he got chilled. And his father, who had also channelled the lightning, found he no longer needed to wear glasses.

Archie continued to study his face in the bathroom mirror. Slaverin' Joe had said one green and one blue eye was a delicacy in the gull world. Now, why should his eyes taste better to a gull than, say, George or Sid's eyes? Then he got to thinking about the strange little hypnotic eyes down at the harbour wall and the sound of wailing and distant marching. The questions kept on coming. Just what had Rufus meant by feeling 'unusual', and why did he find it so hard to remember whether he had swallowed any sea water? Archie could still taste a hint of salt so he filled his cupped hands with tap water and rinsed his mouth. He was reaching for the tap when he heard the crack of static and a burning sensation shot through the tips of every one of his wet fingers.

Chapter Six

When Archie arrived at Westervoe Village School on Monday morning, he found Sid and George leaning against the wheelie bins. Sid was demonstrating a slack tooth. 'I can almost twist it right round.'

George was unimpressed and Sid turned his attention to Archie.

'Did you tell your mum and dad I saved you from drowning yesterday?'

'I wasn't drowning,' Archie told him.

Sid stopped wiggling his tooth. 'I saved you too!'

'I *wasn't* drowning,' Archie insisted.

'You would have drowned if I hadn't followed you down the slipway,' George assured him.

'And me!' Sid added.

Archie was about to protest some more but the bell was ringing. George and Sid joined a mad rush of pupils all wanting to be at the head of their individual class line-up. Archie couldn't be bothered. He was too tired. He'd lain awake the previous night waiting for Rufus to arrive back after driving off in the Land Rover again just after nine o'clock. He still hadn't returned by the time Archie eventually fell asleep sometime around midnight.

This morning Archie couldn't keep his eyes open and the walk along the corridor to his classroom felt like a long trek into the wilderness.

Once seated, he yawned and rested his head on the table he shared with Sid and George. Just for a moment, he told himself, until he regained a little more energy.

Mr Taylor, his teacher, had other ideas. He raised his eyes from the register and enquired, 'What time did you go to your bed last night, Archie Stringweed?'

Archie sat up. 'Nine o'clock, sir.'

'Make it 8.30 tonight,' said Mr Taylor. 'You're the colour of that grey gull on the window sill.'

The entire class strained their necks to look out of the window.

'Sit down,' said Mr Taylor in a pretend grumpy voice. 'You'd think you'd never seen a herring gull before.'

While he carried on marking the register, Archie, Sid and George took another sneaky look at the gull. 'It looks like the one that tried to peck our eyes out,' George whispered.

The gull had been staring out to sea but turned its

head slowly and looked straight at Archie.

'It *is* the same gull,' Sid decided. 'It's following us!'

Mr Taylor closed the register. 'Let us repay a visit to the nine times table.'

There was a collective groan from a handful of pupils, including Archie.

'A beautiful table,' Mr Taylor was saying. 'One of my favourites.' He gave an appreciative smile. 'A mathematical duet. Such harmony.' He swung round on his chair and pointed to a chart on the wall. 'Look at the numbers in the tens column. See how they increase while those in the units column decrease. 18, 27, 36, 45 . . . Who will stand up and recite this numerical poetry?'

Mr Taylor surveyed the class, east to west, north to south, finally stopping at Archie, whose eyes were watering with the effort of suppressing another yawn. His hands were sticky, too, with 'I don't know my tables' nerves, and there was the matter of that gull sitting on the window ledge watching him.

'Up on your feet, Archie,' said Mr Taylor. 'Before you start snoring.'

The class laughed.

Archie stood up, and just as his knees clicked into place there came a knock at the door. Mrs Merriman, the head teacher, breezed in with her wide shapeless skirt flapping around her chunky legs. Because she was always in a hurry, she spoke in short breathless sentences.

'Morning. New girl here. Have you room for one more, Mr Taylor? She's come all the way from London.' A tall thin-faced girl with a long brown pony-tail followed Mrs Merriman's busy strides. Mrs Merriman handed Mr Taylor a folder, spoke quietly to him for a moment and then turned to the class and smiled. 'Make her feel welcome, everyone.' Her skirt gave another flutter as she strode out the door.

'Well,' said Mr Taylor to the thin-faced girl. 'I suppose we should begin with some introductions. Would you care to tell us your name?'

'Ruby,' she said, and her face turned the colour of her name. 'Ruby Larkingale.'

Mr Taylor looked thoughtful. 'I once knew a Ruby. Could play the accordion and crack walnuts with her teeth.' He looked to the class. 'Say hello to Ruby, everyone.'

'Not *another* girl,' George was mumbling to himself. 'We're outnumbered sixteen to ten.'

For Archie, her arrival was good news, particularly since Mr Taylor seemed to have forgotten all about the nine times table. Whoever Ruby was, she had saved him, and as a thank you he returned the small wave she gave to the twenty-five inquisitive children all staring back at her.

Ruby was seated at a table directly in front of Archie, Sid and George.

'Linda and Suzie will keep an eye on you,' Mr Taylor told her. 'They're my eyes and ears.'

'Spies more like,' George said under his breath, but his sourness quickly turned to confusion when Ruby turned, stared at Archie for a moment, then gave him a faint smile.

Linda and Suzie were the bossiest and smartest girls in the class. It was evident Ruby was going to give them a run for their money when she completed an arithmetic paper in record time.

'Well, well,' said an impressed Mr Taylor, 'it must be our Westervoe air.'

At PE Ruby demonstrated a controlled handstand she had learned at a circus workshop. At lunch she had two plates of spaghetti bolognese followed by treacle tart and didn't once have to use a serviette.

There was a lot of interest in the new girl Ruby. So much so that Linda and Suzie stood either side of her like bodyguards, selecting who could and who couldn't talk to her. For those lucky enough to be selected, the questions came fast and furious.

'Have you got any pets?'

'Terrapins and a –'

'Do you have any brothers or sisters?'

'No.'

'Do you like mushrooms?' was someone else's question, but by now Ruby was eyeing up the football game Archie was organising and to Linda and Suzie's surprise she asked the boys if she could join in.

George grumbled something about girls not being able to play football properly, but Archie had already said 'Yes' and Sid saw it as an opportunity for someone else to be stuck in goal for a while.

George continued to mutter ungallant remarks about girls playing football, but Ruby didn't seem to notice. She was far too busy saving goal after goal, and by the time the bell rang for the start of afternoon classes, Sid had invited her to play again. But Archie was exhausted after his late night and he hoped Ruby didn't think he played that badly all the time.

As they stood in line ready to walk back into the school, he glanced over his shoulder and noticed the battered-looking gull loitering close to the wheelie bins. As Mr Taylor had said, it *was* a very ordinary-looking gull, but on the other hand Archie knew for sure that ordinary-looking gulls don't return your stare with a wink.

Chapter Seven

Ever since breaking the Stringweed family curse, Archie had been given new independence by his parents. This included walking back from school alone on condition that he return home by 4.30 p.m. This gave him ample time to go into Sweet Stuff with Sid and George and buy his favourite sweets – chewy lemon eels. When they emerged from the shop, George suggested walking over to the shingle beach next to the museum to skim stones.

'I want to improve my record nine jumps,' he told them.

Archie agreed but Sid seemed unsure. He could hear gulls shrieking in the distance.

'OK,' he said, looking up at the sky. 'But I think we should take turns doing gull watch.'

'You're scared!' George said and he made a noise at the back of his throat that resembled a laugh. 'It's not *us* the gull wants, it's *Archie*!' He curled his mouth into a sneer to reveal a half-chewed liquorice leech stuck to his teeth.

Archie watched the sly way George was looking at him.

'If you're going to pick an argument,' Archie warned, 'I'm going home.'

Sid halted his gull watch. 'No! Don't go home.'

George packed another leech into his mouth. 'No skin off my nose,' he mumbled. 'I've got other friends.'

The potential argument was interrupted by the sound of an approaching car and they stood aside to allow the vehicle to pass through the narrow street. It was a tight squeeze and Archie found himself standing on a large metal grid covering a drain. A piece of thick brown seaweed was poking up out of the drain between his feet and, curiously, it appeared to be moving. He kicked it with the toe of his shoe and he thought he heard a faint squeal as it dropped back out of sight.

Meantime, the approaching car had slowed down. Sitting at the wheel of a white estate was a woman whose mass of blonde curls was partly tamed by a red headband. Beside her in the front passenger seat was Ruby, who gave the boys a small wave of recognition, but her smile was for Archie. George scowled back at her, but Archie didn't notice. He was more concerned with the uncomfortable tingling sensation at the tips of his fingers. It reminded him of the after-effects of being struck by lightning and the static shocks he had been getting lately, but the feeling had gone by the time the boys turned the corner of the museum building and ran on to the shingle beach. They threw their rucksacks on top of an upturned dinghy and skidded down through the pebbles to the water's edge.

George pointed to something moving in the shallow water. 'Hey! I can see a crab. A big one too!' He threw a stone towards it and declared, 'Bang on target.'

Archie and Sid were more interested in looking for flat stones to skim across the water. Although Sid had managed to gather up a handful, Archie couldn't find one suitable stone. They were either too big, too small or not the right shape at all. He dug closer to the waterline and found what at first appeared to be a piece of smooth glass, but when he picked it up he discovered it was in fact a green pebble. What struck him as doubly unusual was the arrow etched across its surface.

He was turning the stone over to examine the underside when George plucked it out of his hand and sent it sailing over the sea.

'Why did you do that?' Archie asked as the stone hit the water and sank. 'It wasn't even a good skimming stone.'

George shrugged his shoulders. 'You sound as sulky as a girl. Maybe that's why you and Sid like playing football with them.'

Sid's mouth opened wide in protest but before he could speak there was a loud echoing squawk.

'Gull alert!' Sid shouted as a grey gull with a fine line of black feathers beneath one wing came sweeping over the museum roof and headed straight towards them. Sid covered his head with his coat and crouched down low. 'Get it away from me!'

But the bird wasn't interested in Sid. It flew at George, who stumbled backwards and slid clumsily on to his bottom. 'Mammy!' he screamed as he curled up into a ball.

Archie covered his face with his hands to protect his eyes. When he dared to peer out through a small gap in his fingers he saw the gull already heading out to sea, George's bag of liquorice leeches dangling from its beak.

'It's gone,' he announced.

'Are you sure?' came Sid's muffled reply.

'Yes,' Archie told him. 'Look!'

Sid emerged out of his coat. George unfurled himself just far enough to take a look at the gull as it came in to land on a large red buoy anchored offshore.

'It attacked *me*!' said George. 'And it's got my leeches!'

'I was right about doing gull watch,' said Sid. 'That gull is following us.' Then something else caught his attention. 'Look at that.'

Mist appeared to be rising up out of the sea in snake-like wisps that were drifting towards them. Even more unusual was the speed at which the wisps were rising and growing thicker. The gull and the red buoy disappeared from sight and a small rowing boat anchored close to shore was quickly swallowed up inside it too. In a matter of seconds they were fully enveloped by the mist. It was like being inside a white tent: slightly claustrophobic, and it made your voice sound muffled. It was quiet too.

Archie was the first to speak. 'Can you hear that?'

'What?' said George.

'Crying.' Archie considered the sound some more. It wasn't crying he could hear but the same high-pitched wailing he had heard down at the harbour when he had seen all those eyes staring up at him.

George shook his head. 'I can't hear anything.'

'Me neither,' whispered Sid, who was looking more and more scared.

The soft silence was unexpectedly broken by the sound of the sea creeping up the pebbles, breaking in small waves close to where they stood.

Sid was completely motionless, but for his eyes, which were nervously darting from left to right. 'I don't like this. I'm going home.'

George agreed and the two of them scrambled up the beach together in a rattle of stones. When they reached the street, George turned left and Sid turned right and disappeared into the mist.

Archie was left alone, listening to the strange wailing coming from somewhere beyond the mist. A cold sickly feeling was churning around in his stomach, telling him he should leave, but he couldn't resist the dancing motion of a clump of seaweed close to his feet and the way it was stretching out towards him, like long green fingers. Even as icy sea water began to seep through his trainers he preferred to watch the seaweed drift over his shoes. Who knows how long he would have stood there if the sound of pebbles rattling close by hadn't roused him from his stupor. Something he couldn't see was on the beach and moving through the mist towards him. His first thought was of rats, and he shook the seaweed from his shoes and scrambled back up the beach, grabbing his bag on the way, and ran on to the safety of the street.

He could barely see further than the hand he held outstretched, ready to protect himself from any unexpected collisions. The only sound to be heard was a delicate tapping on the ground behind him. He turned but could see nothing. Then he heard the delicate tapping again, and a crab with unusually large pincers scuttled over his shoes and disappeared down through the bars of the same drain cover he had stood on earlier. And as if that wasn't odd enough, a voice was calling out, 'We're all cursed!'

Slaverin' Joe's old red pickup emerged out of the mist and he peered at Archie through the open window. 'Nothing can save us now! We're all doomed!'

Archie stood open-mouthed as he watched the pickup drive on. A selection of old rusting lawnmowers, piled up in the back, resembled weird headless skeletons rising from a misty grave.

Archie continued to edge his way along the street and, to his relief, people were at last beginning to loom out of the mist. He didn't mind when he walked straight into the fish shop's delivery bike that had been left propped up against a wall, or when he almost fell over the ice-cream sign outside the post office, because by then he was well on his way home. He passed the library on the corner, turned left and headed on up the hill.

The dense mist had soaked his hair and clothes and an overgrown fuchsia bush brushed his face with its wet leaves. He was wiping his cheeks dry when he felt a movement close behind and he spun round. He could see nothing other than empty whiteness. The beating of wings broke through the eerie silence and stirred the mist above him. He heard the crack of a small hard object hitting the pavement and then it was rattling down the hill towards him. He turned and kept watch on the ground, waiting for the object to appear out of the fog. When it did, he could scarcely believe his eyes. A pale green pebble, with an arrow etched on one side, came to a standstill directly in front of his right foot.

Chapter Eight

Archie had no sooner picked up the pebble and put it in his pocket than the mist began to clear as fast as it had appeared. It sped by as though being sucked out to sea by a giant vacuum cleaner, and by the time he reached Windy Edge it had cleared completely. A blue van was parked outside the gate where the Land Rover usually stood. On its roof was a set of ladders and in white letters on the side of the van were the words 'D.E. Muir & Son, Plumbers'.

Archie kicked off his soggy trainers, left his coat and bag in the hall and walked into the kitchen. His mother was standing by the sink, her arms folded, and she was frowning.

'One minute the drain is blocked, the next it's clear.'

She was explaining this to the plumber, whose head was stuck deep in the cupboard under the kitchen sink. All that was visible of him was a pair of battered white trainers and the bottom half of a dark blue boiler suit.

On the floor around him were bottles of various cleaning fluids, a roll of black refuse sacks and a selection of dried-out paintbrushes in a jam jar.

'I can't find anything wrong,' the plumber was saying. 'Water's draining away. No smell.' He pulled his head out of the cupboard and stood up. 'It's a mystery.'

'It's a nuisance, that's what it is,' Cecille told him.

The plumber began putting the tools away in his bag.

'Could it be a rat in there?' Cecille asked and she gave a shiver of disgust.

The plumber shook his head. 'Never known a rat to come up through a kitchen sink. A toilet maybe, but never a sink. Next time it blocks, ring me and I'll come straight over. Catch it before it clears. Then we'll see what's lurking in there.'

Cecille agreed and the plumber washed his hands and left.

'Where's Rufus?' Archie wanted to know as he spread strawberry jam on a pancake.

Cecille was peering down the plughole of the sink. 'Haven't seen him all afternoon.'

'We got a new girl in our class today,' Archie remarked.

'Oh yes?' said Cecille, who was now sniffing the drain.

'Her name's Ruby Larkingale,' Archie told her. 'She's quite a good goalkeeper.'

'There it goes again!' Cecille announced.

'What?' said Archie.

'That clicking sound. Come over here and listen.'

Archie went and leaned over the sink.

'Why is your hair wet?' Cecille asked.

'Mist,' he answered.

Cecille glanced out the window to an overcast but clear afternoon. She looked at Archie again, shook her head in a confused manner and then returned to the matter in hand.

'Do you hear it clicking?' she asked.

Archie stood up quickly, almost colliding heads with Cecille.

'What do you think it is?' she asked.

He shook his head and began backing away. It wasn't clicking he heard, but the sound of a distant marching army. How could he explain that to his mother when he could hardly believe it himself?

Cecille, meanwhile, had turned on the tap. 'Maybe it's a trapped air bubble.' She watched the water drain away and then a thought occurred to her. 'A new girl in your class, did you say?'

But Archie was already gone, running upstairs to his room with a plate of pancakes in his hand.

He sat down on his bed to examine the green pebble and consider the increasing number of peculiar events.

He held a pancake between his teeth and ripped a page from a small notebook that was lying on his bedside table. With a blunt pencil he began to make a list.

1. *Herring gull following me. Wants to peck my eyes out?*
2. *Sea water. Might have swallowed some? Getting static shocks.*
3. *Eyes on the harbour wall. Feeling sleepy.*
4. *Marching sound at the Point, at the harbour and now the kitchen sink.*
5. *Mist/wailing/mysterious green pebble.*
6. *Crab on the street.*

Conclusion? Must talk to Rufus.

Archie took a bite of the pancake and returned it to the plate. That was the moment his attention was drawn to the weatherscope. The glass globe, which was the size of a large orange, was covered in a fine layer of dust, making the miniature planets inside it appear lacklustre. Looking at it now, it was difficult to believe they had once spun so fast they resembled liquid gold. And the brass base was no longer bright and shiny, but dull and tarnished. He spat on his fingers, ready to clean it, but as he reached for the metal a static spark hit his fingertips and a flash of white light lit up the inside of the weatherscope. For a split second he was blinded by the brightness but when his eyesight cleared he saw that a

51

fine circle of condensation, about the size of a ten pence piece, had collected on top of the globe. Archie dried it with his sleeve but another circle immediately formed. It spread itself over the entire globe and began to wash it. What he saw through the clean glass produced a churning excitement in his stomach. The weatherscope now contained a hint of colour; violet, he thought, but already it was turning to purple and then finally blue, confirming what he already suspected. It was registering curse activity.

Archie went over to a wall cupboard, took a shoebox down from the top shelf and carried it over to his bed. He removed the lid and looked inside at an unusual collection of objects, all of which had been instrumental in the extermination of the Stringweed family curse.

There was a battered old black torch that had seen better days. A rabbit's foot on a gold chain, a long thin gold key and a magnifying glass with a gold-plated surround. A pair of Second World War flying goggles, a flute, a pocket watch and a dagger. He carefully removed the artefacts one by one, hoping for a glimmer of the power each had given him in his battle against the evil tornado, Huigor. Disappointingly, there was not even the slightest sensation of courage when he picked up the snake-handled dagger. Several other items were lying at the bottom of the box, including a chain with a gold hoop engraved with the words *Archie*

Stringweed, Curse Exterminator, and set into this hoop were the two medals he had received from I.C.E. in recognition for breaking the curse of Huigor.

The final item Archie removed from the box was a pure white feather. But this was no ordinary feather. It belonged to a mythical creature he knew to be real. An Icegull. It had fluorescent green eyes and could expand or reduce in size. He recalled how one Icegull in particular, as big as the snowplough Sid's dad drove, had told him that his courage would be called upon again. And now the weatherscope was showng him that time was drawing close.

He was adding the words 'Weatherscope registering curse activity' to his list when the walkie-talkie lying on his bed began to crackle and his mother's voice asked, 'Archie –?'

'I'm starting it now,' he replied without taking his eyes from the weatherscope.

'Would you like some help?'

'No thanks,' he told her. 'Got to go. Over and out.'

But he was far too excited to start his homework. Instead he paced the room wondering what kind of curse activity the weatherscope was registering. Over and over again he stared out the window, looking for Rufus pulling up in the Land Rover. Eventually he pulled off his wet socks and lay down on his bed. Outside, a bird was tramping across the roof and tapping its beak against the tiles. Archie ignored the persistent sound and turned his attention to the times tables wallchart next to his bed. Today he had managed to avoid reciting the nine times table but tomorrow he might not be so lucky. A mass of numbers hovered before him, too many to remember, and other thoughts kept interrupting his concentration. He tried very hard to keep them at bay, but one in particular kept coming back, over and over again.

Why had Ruby smiled at him and not at George and Sid?

Chapter Nine

By the time Archie came downstairs to dinner that evening, it was dark outside. Cecille was dishing up a beef casserole. Jeffrey was home from the bank and standing directly in front of the kitchen TV flicking through the channels. His tie was hanging loose and he was eating a breadstick.

'Is Rufus home?' Archie wanted to know.

Cecille shook her head. 'Rufus went off in the Land Rover this morning. I haven't seen him since.'

'Maybe he's at the Point,' Archie suggested. After all, Maggie had seen Rufus there when out walking her dogs.

'I hope not,' Jeffrey said, without taking his eyes from the TV. 'Going out to the Point in the dark is asking for trouble, especially with equinox high tides due.'

Archie was about to ask what time Rufus had come home the previous night but Jeffrey was watching the long-range weather forecast.

'Good. It's going to stay dry until the end of the week,' he announced. 'If we set off for Edinburgh straight after school on Wednesday, we'll be in plenty of time for the I.C.E. ceremony.'

Cecille was busy draining the boiled potatoes. 'I haven't a thing to wear to the presentation. I think I'll go shopping in Breckwall tomorrow.' She turned to Archie. 'I'll ask Grandma to pick you up from school.'

Just then, the front door slammed.

Archie listened to Rufus kick off his boots and hang up his jacket. He twisted round in his chair as footsteps approached the kitchen but they suddenly veered off down the stairs to the basement.

Cecille returned the casserole to the oven. Meanwhile, Jeffrey almost choked on his breadstick. 'Good grief!' he said. 'Look at that!' He was pointing to the TV screen.

A group of local fishermen were explaining how they had returned empty-handed to harbour from yet another unsuccessful fishing trip. 'There's no fish to be had out there,' one of them said. 'Nothing moving except crabs, and with the biggest claws I've ever seen.'

To prove his point, he held a dead crab up by its enormous claw while another fisherman spread open a ripped net to show the damage the crabs had caused.

A professor of marine biology was then interviewed and he suggested the large number of crabs was most likely a mass migration. The unusually large pincers he put down to an evolutionary development associated with dwindling fish stocks, though he couldn't be absolutely sure. 'A very odd phenomenon indeed,' he conceded.

Archie was reminded of the crab with large pincers he'd seen on the street. He started to mention this but Jeffrey said, 'Shh, listen!' The TV presenter was now introducing someone with local knowledge who had been interviewed earlier that day. Suddenly Slaverin' Joe appeared on the screen above a caption which read 'Joseph Sinclair. Folklore Expert'.

'Folklore expert?' gasped Cecille. 'Since when?'

Joe was wearing his orange coat and red baseball cap. Behind him the grey sea was running fast against the black rocks of the Point.

The interviewer pointed her gloved hand towards the sea. 'So tell us what you think is out there, Mr Sinclair?'

'A curse,' said Joe.

The interviewer smiled. 'A curse?'

But Joe wasn't smiling. 'Seen it with my own eyes. Back in '62. Off the west coast of Ireland. The sea was heaving with eels.'

The interviewer sounded confused. 'And you believe there's a connection between the two?'

'Where there's unusual marine activity, there's

mermaids. And where there's mermaids? There's trouble.'

'Mermaids?'

Joe looked straight to camera. 'Stay away from the sea around Westervoe. Don't go out to the Point, and if I was you?' He leaned closer to the camera. 'Don't go anywhere near the caves.' The shadows beneath his eyes looked as black as the rocks as he growled, 'They're cursed!'

Archie glanced at his parents. Cecille's tongue had come to a standstill at the corner of her mouth. Jeffrey's unfinished breadstick was still clamped between his teeth. Neither of them moved.

The interviewer, however, was still smiling. 'Well, it appears the advice from Mr Sinclair is don't get in the way of curses . . . or mermaids for that matter . . . and stay away from the caves if you know what's good for you.'

The report finished and they were all still getting over Joe's ominous warning when the next news item was introduced. A terrier appeared on the screen wearing a tartan bow tie and barking a recognisable version of 'The Good Ship Lollipop'.

Jeffrey switched the TV off. Cecille looked worried. 'I wonder when that interview with Joe was recorded?'

'This morning,' a voice announced from behind them.

Rufus walked towards the table and sat down. He smelt of soap and his hair was damp and looked as if he had just run his fingers through it.

Cecille went to the stove and took the casserole dish out again. Jeffrey took off his jacket, hung it on the back of the chair and sat down next to Rufus.

'So what do you make of this curse business? Joe's not serious, is he?'

'Joe knows nothing, but something's going on out there.'

'What do you mean, "something"?'

'I took the plane up last night around sunset. Flew beyond the Point. Saw a dark shadow moving beneath the sea. Looks like a shoal of fish, but it doesn't flit and change direction. Slow, too, and steady.'

'What do you think it was?' Jeffrey asked and he rested his elbows on the table, eager to hear Rufus's opinion.

'Mermaids!' Cecille said with a laugh.

Rufus didn't laugh. 'Joe was making a wild guess about what is going on but he happened to get it right. There are mermaids around the caves.'

Cecille gasped and almost dropped the plate of stew she was passing to Rufus. 'You have got to be joking!'

Rufus shook his head. 'They're not mermaids as we think of them. These are ugly-looking things and vicious too. Unfortunately, Joe's warning is going to encourage every foolhardy idiot to go and take a look for themselves.' He put his head into his hands. 'A recipe for disaster.'

Archie saw his chance to question Rufus.

'But you've been out to the Point. George's Auntie Maggie saw you there.'

Rufus looked at him. 'I said "every foolhardy idiot" will go out there. I know what I'm doing. Something dangerous is going on in the caves. Something other people don't understand.'

'Slaverin' Joe said it had to do with a curse. Is he right about that too?' Archie asked.

Rufus nodded. 'Afraid so.'

Cecille sat down at the table and announced, 'Well, whatever it is, this curse isn't anything to do with us.' She expected Rufus to agree, but he was staring down at the table, drawing on the slab of butter with his fork. And when Jeffrey said, 'We battled Huigor and won. Surely we're off the hook where curses are concerned?' Rufus continued with his doodling.

But when Archie asked, 'If mermaids and fish aren't making the shadow in the sea, then what is?' Rufus raised his head and showed renewed interest. 'Not sure yet,' he replied. 'Been charting it for a couple of days and it's kept a steady course.'

Archie thought about his list of unusual occurrences and the weatherscope and the sound of the marching army. 'It's heading towards Westervoe, isn't it?'

'Of course not!' Cecille said.

But Rufus nodded his head and said, 'Yes, I'm afraid it's heading this way.'

An air of anxiety could be felt in the kitchen following Slaverin' Joe's TV appearance and Rufus's confirmation that whatever was moving beneath the sea's surface was heading their way.

Cecille tried easing the tension by dishing up a chocolate sponge she had bought that day from the bakery. Archie had two helpings and then got up from the table to pour himself a glass of water. As his hand touched the tap, a sharp pain speared the tips of his fingers and he cried out.

Everyone stopped eating. Cecille turned round in her chair. 'What's wrong?'

'Static,' said Archie and he shook the pain from his fingers.

Jeffrey went back to eating his pudding, but Rufus sat watching Archie.

Cecille stood up from the table. 'Where did you pick up static?'

Archie was aware of Rufus's eyes on him as he said, 'Felt it since Sunday.'

Cecille cautiously stretched her fingers towards the tap and, finding no static, poured Archie a glass of water. Jeffrey, meantime, was saying, 'Rufus, could you show me on a map where you saw this shadow?'

'Depends on the scale of the map,' Rufus told him. 'But I can give an approximate sighting.'

'Then let's all go down to the study,' said Jeffrey. 'I've got a good atlas down there.'

'You three carry on,' Cecille told them. 'Give me a shout when you're ready.'

Rufus and Archie followed Jeffrey downstairs and Cecille began clearing the table. She was about to pick up the pudding bowls when she heard the softest tapping at the window. Large raindrops were running down the glass.

'So much for dry weather till the weekend,' she muttered.

She crossed to the window, ready to place a tea towel along the sill in preparation for the usual leaks, and was surprised to find water already trickling and bubbling in under the window frame as though fighting to get into the house.

An atlas lay open on Jeffrey's study table. Rufus was bent over it, closely examining the coastline round Westervoe. His face wore a look of concentration as he traced the map with his index finger while Jeffrey and Archie stood either side of him waiting for his verdict.

'There!' Rufus finally announced, and he tapped the map with his finger. 'That's where I saw the shadow. About two miles south of Moss Rock.'

'And how big was this shadow?' Jeffrey wanted to know.

'I'd say forty metres, top to tip. Maybe half that in width.'

'That's big!' said Archie.

'Is it a shipping hazard?' Jeffrey wanted to know.

Rufus shook his head. 'No. It's definitely organic.'

Jeffrey lowered his voice. 'I think we should play this down. I don't want Cecille worrying about curses. It's only three months since we got rid of Huigor.'

Rufus was happy to agree. 'Of course. Anyway, nothing's certain yet.'

He had no sooner said this, than Cecille appeared at the study door wearing the strangest expression. In her hand was the butter dish and she held it out towards Rufus. 'What's this?' she asked.

'Cecille?' said Jeffrey, and he rolled his eyes in a gesture of incredulity. 'It's the butter!'

'No,' she said. '*This.*'

She was pointing to the doodle Rufus had drawn with the fork. Jeffrey and Archie leaned closer for a better look and saw the drawing resembled a jellyfish but within the mass of tentacles there was a body and on this body was a head.

Rufus hesitated before revealing, 'It's a Jellat.'

'A what?' said Jeffrey.

Rufus folded his arms across his chest and began his explanation. 'Jellats are deep ocean creatures and only seen near the sea's surface when curse activity is present. They are invertebrates. Similar in appearance to jellyfish, except their tentacles resemble seaweed and they have two perfectly round eyes. On the underside of these tentacles are small globules that glow in the dark. Their sting is contained within a set of narrow cream tentacles, rather like spaghetti. The sting is not usually deadly but their teeth –'

'Is this a mermaid?' Cecille interrupted.

Rufus looked apologetic. 'Admittedly, it's not a good likeness. Can never get the detail with room temperature butter. But the answer to your question is "yes", this is what is being referred to as a mermaid but is, in fact, a Jellat. Unfortunately, they look even uglier than that.'

'*That's* a Jellat?' said Archie. It wasn't just the drawing that surprised him but what Rufus had said about their eyes and the mass of swirling tentacles that looked just like seaweed. In his excitement he blurted out, 'I've seen a Jellat.'

Three adult voices simultaneously said, '*What?*' And three sets of adult eyes all stared down at him. Rufus looked particularly interested.

'When? Where?'

Archie gulped and looked at each of them in turn, saying, 'At the harbour. On Sunday. When I was fishing.'

Jeffrey shot a cautious glance at Cecille, who just happened to be shooting a cautious glance back. Archie recognised it as the kind of look they used when they were preparing to be overprotective and, because he didn't want his fishing trips at the harbour to be cancelled, he said, 'Well . . . I think I saw a Jellat.'

Cecille was happy to accept this explanation and she smiled with relief. 'Honestly, Archie. You and your imagination.'

Jeffrey looked equally relieved. 'I think it's time to stop all talk of curses.' He closed the atlas firmly and said, 'We're filling Archie's head with a lot of nonsense.'

Cecille agreed. 'After all, curses have nothing more to do with us.'

'Absolutely nothing,' Jeffrey agreed. 'Isn't that so, Rufus?'

But Rufus was otherwise occupied. He had a well-sharpened pencil in his hand and was carefully drawing a set of very sharp teeth on to the Jellat.

The rain continued to fall all evening. It stomped the ground around the house like heavy boots and fell down the living room chimney, hissing and spitting on the hot coals. When Archie heard knocking at the window, he opened the curtains to find long fingers of water slapping the glass and drumming against the window ledge. By the time he climbed upstairs to bed a small damp patch had appeared on the ceiling above the window. As he stood looking up at it, he heard a knock at his bedroom door and Rufus popped his head into the room.

Archie couldn't wait to tell him about the weather-scope. 'Look. It's registering curse activity!'

But Rufus's interest was elsewhere. 'Are you sure you saw Jellats down at the harbour?'

Archie hesitated. He realised he couldn't be absolutely sure because he had never seen a Jellat before. All he had to go on was Rufus's butter drawing.

'I definitely saw hundreds of eyes peering out of seaweed.'

Rufus was pondering this reply when Archie said, 'When do I get to exterminate Jellats?'

Rufus walked into the room. 'Not so fast! This curse activity is highly unusual. More research is needed. In the meantime, I don't want you taking things into your own hands. Your job is to keep the artefacts safe.'

A drop of water fell from the ceiling.

'You'd better find a bucket,' Rufus told him as a drip landed on the carpet.

Archie said he would rather discuss curse activity, but

Rufus was insistent. 'If you're going to be a good curse exterminator you must learn to be patient. Now fetch a bucket, please.'

Once Archie had left the room and was running down the stairs, Rufus positioned himself beneath the leak and caught a falling drip in his palm. He inspected it closely before crossing to the bedside table and looking into the blue-tinged weatherscope. He drummed his fingers thoughtfully on the table, accidentally knocking a piece of paper to the floor, which he picked up and began to read – it was Archie's list.

Cecille, meanwhile, was telling Archie she didn't have a spare bucket for the leak in his room. The only one she had was being used to soak tea towels. But then Jeffrey remembered seeing an old white milking pail in the junk room. He emptied it of the polystyrene chips that Cecille was sure would come in handy one day, and they all trooped up to the attic.

Rufus was nowhere to be seen.

'I wonder where he went,' Archie said.

Jeffrey looked up at the damp patch on the ceiling. 'Must be a loose roof tile.' He placed the bucket on the floor and announced, 'That should do the job!'

There was the ring of a raindrop hitting the inside of the bucket, closely followed by the sound of a car speeding away. Archie hurried to the window in time to catch a glimpse of the Land Rover lights racing down the hill into the darkness. He had a good idea where Rufus was going and Cecille did too.

'Whatever is going on at the Point is nothing to do with us!' she assured him before leaving the room with Jeffrey.

Archie agreed. Curse activity had nothing to with his parents, but then again it had everything to do with him. He went over to his bed and pulled the shoebox out from underneath it. As he sat on the floor looking at the collection of artefacts inside the box, he made a vow. 'I am an International Curse Exterminator and *I* am going to break this curse.' With that, another drip rang out from inside the bucket like a small metallic cheer.

Chapter Ten

Archie had tried his best to stay awake until Rufus arrived back at Windy Edge. He had thought about following him on his bike, but he was put off by the heavy rain thundering against the roof tiles. Instead he snuggled up into his blue quilt and fell asleep to the sound of drips hitting the inside of the pail. It was the first sound he was conscious of when he awoke the following morning.

He got out of bed and looked through the window to the watery outline of the Land Rover parked outside the gate. If Rufus had discovered anything new about curse activity the previous night, then Archie wanted to know before leaving for school.

He quickly turned from the window and almost tripped over the pail. As he steadied it with his hands, a drip of water fell from the ceiling and landed on the back of his neck. He felt it race down his back, tickling each of his vertebrae in turn until it came to a rest at the bottom of his spine. He wiped it away but was amazed to find that it quickly reformed into a large drop on the tip of his index finger. He spent the next ten seconds passing this single drop from one fingertip to another until they had all been touched by it. As he looked down at the drop now sitting on the tip of his thumb, he squeezed it firmly into his palm and rubbed his hands together. When he reopened his hands, the water was already reforming into a single drop and this time Archie flicked it into the pail of water. To his surprise it burst, leaving a small pool of colour on the surface of the water.

Archie went over to the list lying on his bedside table and added to it the words 'Drop of water fell from ceiling on to my spine. Wouldn't burst.' At the top of the page, in capital letters, he wrote 'LIST OF UNUSUAL OCCURRENCES', then he looked inside the weatherscope for further evidence of curse activity. Not only was the globe blue from the night before, but the planets inside it had tilted to the right and were vibrating in tiny see-saw movements.

Archie quickly pulled on his clothes and ran down the attic stairs. Even before he reached the first floor landing he could hear Jeffrey's voice drifting up from the kitchen.

'. . . I don't think it's reason enough for Rufus to visit the doctor . . .'

'It wasn't just a nightmare,' Cecille was insisting. 'Rufus was delirious last night. I could hear him mumbling nonsense about fire and shadows. Which reminds me, have you noticed the shadows under his eyes?'

'Probably just tired from all these late nights,' Jeffrey decided, although he didn't sound too sure.

Cecille wasn't convinced either. 'Then what about the bloodstains in the bathroom sink this morning?' Archie heard the fridge door opening and Cecille saying, 'Let's hope Rufus didn't pick up a tropical disease on his world travels. We could all get infected.'

Archie walked into the warm kitchen. It was filled with the sounds of the TV and rain hitting the window-panes and water bubbling under the leaking sill.

Jeffrey was dressed ready for work, and was spooning cornflakes from a bowl into his mouth. 'Morning, Archie,' he said before turning his attention back to ScotTV news.

'Has Rufus had breakfast?' Archie asked.

Jeffrey glanced at Cecille, who quickly looked away and began rearranging the fridge contents.

'Rufus is still in bed,' Jeffrey told him.

Archie sniffed. 'I can smell kippers.'

Cecille pulled her head out of the fridge and looked at him as though he was slightly mad. 'Kippers? On a Tuesday?'

Jeffrey was now flicking between the news channels and Archie tried his best to sound only casually interested as he asked, 'Anything more on curses?'

'I don't want to hear anything more about curses,' Cecille replied. 'Someone else can sort it out this time.' Then she stuck her head back inside the fridge and said, 'There's an egg in here. "Use by 20th March." Anyone want it?'

Archie was eating the boiled egg very, very slowly while nibbling at a slice of toast. He didn't know how much longer he could postpone leaving for school. If only Rufus would get out of bed so he could show him his list and discuss any new developments. But perhaps he was too ill. Bloodstains in the bathroom sink didn't sound too good.

Archie's slow eating pace became too much for Jeffrey, who announced, 'I'm leaving in five minutes. Ready or not. Environmental Health is visiting the bank this morning. A rat was spotted in the basement yesterday.'

Archie got up from the table and reluctantly climbed the stairs. Curse activity was approaching and, if Huigor was anything to go by, it was as unpredictable as the weather. Archie reasoned that it made sense to be prepared for the unexpected, which is why on reaching his attic room he opened the box of artefacts. He couldn't possibly take the dagger to school, and the flying goggles, magnifying glass, torch and flute might attract attention. He decided on the key because it was small and easy to conceal, but as he slipped it into his trouser pocket beside the green pebble, he felt a pang of uncertainty. It was against I.C.E. regulations to carry artefacts unless to break a specific curse, but he reassured himself by saying the key was probably the safest of all to carry around.

Cecille was waiting in the hall. She was wearing a raincoat and holding a large umbrella in her hand. 'Don't forget we're all meeting at Grandma's tonight for one of her roast dinners. She'll pick you up from school,' she reminded Archie.

Jeffrey opened the front door and the hall was filled with the hush of heavy rain.

'So much for a dry weather forecast until the weekend,' he said.

Cecille opened the umbrella and they all ran towards the Land Rover. Archie climbed in the back and was pulling the door shut when he noticed a small cloud hovering above the house. A wispy tendril was reaching down from it and touching a loose tile above his bedroom, at the exact spot where drips of water were falling from the ceiling into the bucket.

Chapter Eleven

Archie was the last in his class to arrive at Wester-voe School that morning. The moment he walked into the classroom he could sense the excitement. The hub of activity was the table he shared with Sid and George and the topic of conversation was Slaverin' Joe's appearance the previous evening on TV. George was busy exaggerating the size of the crab claws and claiming some were large enough to cut off a man's arm.

Then someone said they'd heard that Slaverin' Joe had once bitten off a kitten's head and boiled it to make soup. There were gasps of horror and laughs of dis-belief as the noise level continued to rise. Everyone seemed to have something to say about Slaverin' Joe or mermaids or curses. Everyone, that is, except Ruby, who was sitting at her desk, head down, engrossed in a book.

The class was still in uproar by the time the door

swung open and Mr Taylor entered. Without saying a word he walked to his desk, placed his leather briefcase on the floor and stood looking at them. Sensing trouble ahead everyone sat down at their desks. Ruby closed her book and folded her arms while Mr Taylor looked and waited. When he could hear the sound of the raindrops on the window, he said, 'Good morning.'

The entire class replied in a well-rehearsed drawl, 'Good morning, Mr Taylor.'

'Is everyone present this morning?' he asked.

There was much rustling and looking around until it was agreed that, yes, everyone was present, except William, who had yet another chest infection.

Mr Taylor began. 'I hope you're all listening very carefully, because I intend to say this only once.'

Everyone nodded to show they were listening carefully.

'There's been a lot of silly talk this morning about curses and –'

Someone sniggered.

Mr Taylor's watchful eyes flashed across to George for a commanding second before continuing. 'There are no such things as curses or mermaids. It is extremely irresponsible for anyone to suggest otherwise. They do not exist in the same way as aliens do not exist. Therefore, there is no need for anybody to go wandering to the caves beyond the Point. All you will find are extremely dangerous tides, owing to the equinox on Friday. I ask you to stay well away from the sea at this time and put all thought of mermaids and curses out of your heads. Do I make myself clear?'

Everyone was saying yes, though not necessarily meaning so. Particularly George, whose eyes had lit up, and, barely moving his lips, he whispered to Archie, 'Let's go out to the Point on Saturday.'

But Archie wasn't listening. He was looking at Ruby. Her arms were still folded and she was maintaining the same upright position she had held during Mr Taylor's announcement, but the significant difference between her and the rest of the class was that she had the look of someone for whom the sighting of a mermaid came as no surprise at all.

Chapter Twelve

Archie could feel a growing unease. Ever since the drip of water from his bedroom ceiling had trickled down his spine he felt as though his senses were on high alert, and he had the overwhelming feeling that something was about to happen. On two occasions he thought he saw out of the corner of his eye a watery figure darting past the classroom window. Yet when he looked outside he could see nothing but the relentless rain that was now exploding against the window like a Catherine wheel.

Mr Taylor got up from his desk to inspect the stream of water pouring on to the window sill.

'Archie!' he announced. 'Would you please report a broken drainpipe to the janitor. Take Ruby with you and make sure you both change into your outdoor shoes. Put on your coats, too.'

The janitor's office was on the other side of the playground. It was no more than a small storeroom and, although it contained a small table and a chair, it was stacked floor to ceiling with boxes of toilet tissue, paper hand-towels and mops and buckets. Mr Petrie, the janitor, looked up from his newspaper as Archie and Ruby walked in.

'We've come to report a flood,' Archie told him.

'Floods are not my department,' he said. 'You'd better speak to him up there,' and he pointed through a window to the sky.

Archie looked up at the watery glass. Was it his imagination or had a liquid hand just wiped the rain from the window? And was that a skull made of rain-water that seemed to be peering in at him?

He felt Ruby nudge him. 'Isn't that so, Archie?'

'What?' he asked.

'We want to report a broken drainpipe outside Mr Taylor's window.'

Archie nodded. 'There's water everywhere.'

'I've only got one pair of hands,' Mr Petrie moaned. 'And they're not plumber's hands.' He began scratching at a red rash on the back of one hand. 'Besides, I'm not going to get a plumber at this short notice. I suppose I'll just have to get Joe.'

'Do you mean Slaverin' Joe?' Archie asked.

Mr Petrie stopped itching. 'His name is Mr Joseph Sinclair. But maybe he's too busy being a TV celebrity.' He puffed out his chest. 'Mermaids, indeed –'

'Perhaps mermaids do exist,' Ruby interrupted.

Archie stared at her. Mr Petrie was staring too.

'Have you ever seen a mermaid?' he asked.

'Might have,' she replied.

Mr Petrie wasn't sure how to respond to this remark. 'You're new, aren't you? What's your name?'

'Ruby Larkingale.'

'Where you living?'

'Ormleigh House.'

This surprised both Archie and Mr Petrie, because Ormleigh House was the biggest and possibly the oldest house in Westervoe. It was also supposed to be haunted.

Mr Petrie stood up and pulled back his shoulders. 'Well, Miss Ruby Larkingale of Ormleigh House. You go back and tell your teacher that I have everything under control.'

Archie glanced back at the window. There was no sign of a watery hand or skull, just the persistent rain on the glass, and he told himself it must have been a trick of the light. Mr Petrie returned to his crossword as Archie and Ruby headed back outside.

They covered their heads with their arms to protect themselves from the downpour and ran towards the school entrance. A river of water was cascading down the playground from the broken drainpipe and they took a running jump over it. Ruby jumped again just for fun, but Archie was looking towards the drainpipe. The water pouring from it resembled a long arm with fingers knocking against the window, and this time it wasn't a trick of the light.

He caught up with Ruby inside the cloakroom.

'I don't think I like Mr Petrie very much,' she announced as she pulled off her coat and wet shoes.

But Archie's thoughts were elsewhere. 'Have you really seen a mermaid?' he asked.

Ruby looked at him as though considering this question, but her reply surprised him. 'How does Mr Petrie know Slaverin' Joe's not telling the truth?' Her eyes narrowed. 'If I could put a curse on anybody, I'd put it on Mr Petrie.'

'Don't!' Archie said. 'Curses can be dangerous!'

He half expected her to burst out laughing, but instead she took a step closer and said, 'My father was eaten by a lion in the jungle after a witch doctor put a curse on it.'

Archie could only stare as he imagined the scenario.

'I'd rather you didn't tell anyone,' she said, returning his stare.

Archie nodded. 'OK.'

'Anyway,' she said, suddenly returning to the original subject, 'they're not really mermaids. They're actually a type of jellyfish called . . .'

. . . Jellats, Archie thought to himself as Ruby spoke

the words.

Then she changed the subject again. 'What's it like having two different coloured eyes? Is your vision the same out of each eye?'

Archie nodded, but returned to the important question. 'So have you seen a Jellat?'

But, infuriatingly, Ruby didn't answer. Instead she just smiled before skipping away in the direction of the classroom, leaving her wet things dripping all over the floor.

Archie looked down at his own feet. Water was spreading out from the soles of his trainers across the tiles and there was that tingly feeling in his fingers again, which he had come to recognise as curse influence. Only this time he could feel it in his toes as well.

Chapter Thirteen

Archie couldn't make up his mind about Ruby. She had been quite prepared to tell him about the Jellats and how her father had been killed by a cursed lion, and yet he got the feeling she was hiding something. He thought back to Monday morning and her first day at school. He thought about the smile she had given him and came to the conclusion it was the kind of smile given by someone who had a secret. In which case, what did she know? He was so engrossed in this thought that the afternoon passed quickly without any more strange occurrences.

But shortly before the end-of-day bell, a cold prickly sensation ran up his spine and entered his fingers and toes. He looked around the room, trying to find the source of this activity, and caught a glimpse of a shadow rippling along the skirting board like a moray eel. He lost sight of it behind the fish tank, but it reappeared on the floor and he watched it slip under the door to take up refuge in the darkness of the art store cupboard.

Archie kept his eyes fixed on the cupboard. His first instinct was to look inside, but Mr Taylor kept it permanently locked. 'It stops things mysteriously disappearing and then reappearing in other classrooms,' he always maintained.

The cupboard being locked was not a problem for Archie, since he had the gold key. He could feel it now, lying in his pocket next to the pebble. The problem was finding an opportunity to unlock the door, but it wouldn't be that afternoon, because Grandma Stringweed was picking him up from school. Frustratingly, it would have to wait until the following day.

'Make sure you take your worksheets home,' Mr Taylor was now saying. 'I want everyone to know the nine times table tomorrow morning. Anyone who doesn't, will write it out by hand five times.'

George was using the flurry of activity as an opportunity to organise a trip out to the caves. Ruby spun round in her chair and George gave her a 'What's it to you?' look that made her turn away again.

Sid told George there was no way he was going to the caves. Archie was still staring at the cupboard, but he agreed.

'I'm not going either.'

'No sense of adventure,' George sneered. 'You Stringweeds are all the same.'

Ruby looked over her shoulder again but George was too busy counting loose change in his pocket to notice.

When the 3.30 bell finally rang at 3.33, Archie held back till last, hoping for a telltale glimpse of a shadow on the move. He was still stalling for time when Mrs Merriman, the head teacher, strode into the room.

'Can I have a quick word with you, Mr Taylor?' she asked and Archie was ushered out the door.

By the time he walked into the cloakroom, George had made a discovery. 'I've forgotten my worksheet!' He looked at Sid. 'If I gave you . . .?'

'No!' Sid told him. 'Get it yourself.'

'Fifty pence?' said George.

Sid hesitated. 'OK. But I want the money up front.'

George placed the coin in Sid's palm. 'Be quick, will you? I'm in a hurry.'

Archie was in a hurry too. With his mother out shopping and his father still at work, he would finally have a chance to show Rufus the List of Unusual Occurrences.

Chapter Fourteen

Archie was standing slumped against a wall inside Grandpa Stringweed's garage. He was feeling annoyed because he'd been back from school for over an hour and the folded-up List of Unusual Occurrences was still in his hand, ready to show Rufus. But Rufus had been otherwise occupied, talking to Ezekiel Arbuthnott and Grandpa about ratchets, dynamos and the price of oil. The three of them were now staring at an old floral sheet covering something large that stood on the floor.

'An aeroplane is all very well,' Grandpa was telling Rufus. 'But it's not convenient, is it? And you can't rely on borrowing Jeffrey's Land Rover every time you want to go out for a drive.' He pulled the floral sheet away to reveal a motorbike and sidecar. 'It's taxed and insured and the engine's fine. Is it of any use to you?'

Rufus was nodding enthusiastically. 'Yes!'

'What it needs is a good long run on the open road,'

Grandpa explained, and he couldn't hide the regret in his voice as he added, 'I'm just not up to it.'

'You could take this beauty all the way to the moon on a single tank of petrol,' Ezekiel told Rufus.

'To the moon and back!' Grandpa added.

Rufus leaned forward to inspect the tread on the front tyre and as his hair parted Archie saw an old silvery scar on the back of his neck, but next to it was a fresh cut, deep and raw, that looked as if it had been made by the claw of a large animal.

Archie stared at the leg of lamb Grandpa was carving at the dining room table. The blood was oozing out on to the plate, reminding him of the bloodstains on the bathroom sink and man-eating lions and the cut on Rufus's neck. When Grandma Stringweed set a dish of Yorkshire puddings on the table, he couldn't help but imagine they were empty eye sockets picked clean by gulls or Slaverin' Joe's nostrils. He didn't feel hungry after that.

'Did anyone see last night's news report?' Grandma asked when all the plates had been served with meat and veg. 'What do you think of Joe being referred to as a folklore expert?'

'He's not an expert on anything,' Cecille snapped. 'Somebody should tell him to stop making a fool of himself.'

Cecille's unexpected surly mood produced an uncomfortable silence, but Ezekiel smoothed over the tension by saying, 'I agree Joe's no expert but he's certainly got plenty of tales to tell. Wouldn't say they're all true. Likes to exaggerate a bit. Maintains an ancestor of his was the last witch in Scotland to be hanged and he insists his mother had sixth sense.'

'What's sixth sense?' Archie asked Ezekiel.

'I suppose she could see and sense things other people can't.'

'Like ghosts?' Archie asked.

Ezekiel nodded. 'Joe once told me a story about his mother going to visit a neighbour who had been ill for quite some time. As she walked up the path, the woman appeared at the door looking remarkably well and invited her in. Moments later she said she was feeling cold and went upstairs to get her shawl. Well, Joe's mother sat and waited, but eventually she went up the stairs to look for her, thinking she might have taken ill again. She noticed a light shining from under a bedroom door and she knocked and went in. There was the woman lying in her bed, with her family gathered around her. She had been dead since early that morning.'

The phone rang and everyone jumped with fright. They were still laughing nervously when Grandpa Stringweed returned from answering the call, but his troubled expression made them all turn serious.

'What's wrong, Dad?' Jeffrey asked.

'It's the police,' Grandpa told him. 'Someone's just tried breaking into the bank.'

Chapter Fifteen

Jeffrey, Cecille, Ezekiel and Archie all piled into the Land Rover while Rufus wheeled the motorbike out of the garage, looking barely recognisable in Grandpa's waxed coat and crash helmet.

'I'll meet you at Windy Edge,' Jeffrey told him before pulling the Land Rover door shut. 'Can't think for the life of me what bank robbers are after,' he said as he started the engine. 'There's no money in Westervoe.' He shook his head in disbelief and accelerated through a deep puddle lying at the end of the drive.

During the short drive from Breckwall to Westervoe, Archie kept turning round in his seat. He was watching the motorbike headlight disappear then reappear around bends in the road. He could hear the rain hammering on the roof and the rattle of the Land Rover engine, but he could also hear the drone of the bike's engine, even though it was a long way off.

'Why is Rufus riding the bike back in this weather?'

Cecille was saying. 'We could have given him a lift.'

The motorbike headlight suddenly raced up and illuminated the inside of the car.

'A man like Rufus needs his independence,' Ezekiel said.

There followed an unspoken agreement that this was indeed the case and, as if to prove the point, Rufus overtook them in a blaze of light and a wash of water thrown up from the side of the road.

By the time Jeffrey dropped Ezekiel off at his cottage and drove up to Windy Edge, Rufus was parked and waiting.

'Can I come to the bank with you?' Archie asked.

'Probably not a good idea,' Jeffrey told him as he performed a three-point turn. 'Especially if the bank turns out to be a crime scene.'

Archie imagined blue flashing lights and detectives, and maybe even an armed response unit surrounding the bank, yet here he was, an I.C.E. medallist, left at home holding a foil plate of lukewarm lamb and vegetables Grandma Stringweed had given him. He stood on the doorstep thinking it just wasn't fair as he listened to the Land Rover speed back down the hill.

He closed the door and wandered into the kitchen. Cecille was reading a white card that she had taken out of a matching envelope. 'There must have been a second post this afternoon,' she said.

Archie put the foil parcel of food down on the table and stood beside her to read the card.

International Curse Exterminators
cordially invite you to
an evening presentation
to be held at their Edinburgh headquarters
on Wednesday 19th March
6.30–8 p.m.

Refreshments will be provided. Rubber-soled shoes
should be worn when inside the building.

(Full address and map are printed on the back
of this invitation.)

Cecille turned the card over and a small red cross on the map marked the location of the I.C.E. headquarters. It advised:

Please ring bell for the Carthusian Historical Society
The Royal Mile
Edinburgh

Cecille looked disappointed as she examined the invitation. 'I don't think my new shoes are rubber-soled.' She was still considering the shoe problem when the phone rang.

'I'll get it!' said Archie. He was hoping Jeffrey had

changed his mind and was calling to say he would pick him up and take him down to the crime scene.

It was Ruby's voice he heard. 'What are you doing after school on Thursday?'

Archie was so surprised that his mind went completely blank.

'Would you like to come for tea?' Ruby was now asking. 'Olivia says it's fine by her.'

'Olivia?'

'My mother.'

Archie was thinking he didn't know anyone else who called their parents by their Christian name when Ruby said, 'Do you want to call back after you've checked with your mother?' which made Archie feel about five years old.

'No, I don't have to check with Cecille,' he told her. 'Thursday's good. Thanks.'

'You're welcome,' she said and hung up.

He was replacing the handset when Cecille walked by in a great hurry. 'Who was that?'

'Ruby, the new girl,' he said as he watched Cecille run up the stairs. 'I've been invited to tea. On Thursday.'

'That's nice,' she replied from the top landing. 'Do you have anything in common?'

'Jellats,' Archie muttered to himself. 'She knows about Jellats,' and he said it as though he couldn't quite believe it himself.

Chapter Sixteen

Jeffrey and Rufus had been at the bank for almost an hour. Archie pressed his nose against his bedroom window, listening for the approaching Land Rover. Instead he heard the sound of the relentless rain and Cecille's voice speaking to him through the walkie-talkie.

'Archie? Would you come down here, please?'

Something in the way she spoke, as though she didn't want to be overheard, made him curious.

By the time he reached the creaky stair, third from the bottom, he knew something was wrong. Not because the normally loud TV had been turned down low but because Cecille was standing with her back to him and peering round the door into the kitchen. The walkie-talkie was still in her hand.

'What is it?' he asked.

She looked at him over her shoulder. 'On the window ledge. Come and see,' and she stood aside so he might take a closer look.

Archie found himself staring at his own reflection, but then another set of eyes blinked. A rain-soaked herring gull was watching him from outside the window.

'At first I thought it was just resting,' Cecille told him. 'But it just keeps standing there, staring at me. Even when I knocked on the glass it didn't show the slightest reaction. It's creepy.'

Archie moved towards the window and the gull began to retch.

Cecille turned away. 'It's going to be sick!'

The bird was stretching and retracting its neck. Archie wasn't too keen on watching it, but then again its reappearance was too much of a coincidence. Sid had been right. This gull *was* following him and he wanted to find out why. He also wanted to know if it was friend or foe.

'Tell me when it's over,' Cecille was saying, and she placed the palms of her hands over her ears and began humming to herself as she walked out into the hall.

Archie leaned closer to the windowpane just as the bird spilled the contents of its beak. Seconds later it gave a loud echoing cry and flew away.

Archie continued to stare out of the window. He was conscious of the usual familiar household noises, but there was another sound. It was a persistent and loud beat coming up through the kitchen sink from an army on the march, and he felt sure it was connected in some way to the gull's visit. What else could explain the green pebble that had fallen from its beak and was now lying on the window sill?

Cecille stopped humming. 'Is the gull gone?'

Archie was excused from answering because the front door opened and Jeffrey and Rufus walked in. There was a lot of noise and activity in the hall, including Cecille's inquisitive voice asking questions. Archie slid open the window and using a sheet of kitchen paper he picked up the pebble and put it in his trouser pocket. He had just closed the window when everyone walked into the kitchen. Cecille looked relieved to see the gull was gone.

She switched on the kettle then turned to Jeffrey and Rufus. 'Tell me everything that happened at the bank.'

'Not much to tell,' said Jeffrey. 'The alarm was ringing when we got there and a couple of policemen were standing around waiting. I opened up the bank and as far as we could see there was no sign of a break-in.'

Cecille looked disappointed. 'That's it?'

Jeffrey nodded. Then his eyes flicked across to Rufus. 'But there was evidence of disturbance down in the strongroom.'

Cecille's eyes were darting back and forth between

Jeffrey and Rufus. 'What kind of disturbance?'

'My safe deposit box was open,' Rufus explained.

'I don't understand,' said Cecille. 'If there was no break-in . . .' Her voice tailed off in confusion.

Rufus pulled up a chair and sat down at the table. 'I was in the strong room earlier today. I told the police that maybe I hadn't shut the door to the safe properly.'

Something in the hesitant way Rufus spoke made Cecille ask, 'Is that what you think happened?'

Rufus pulled the key from his trouser pocket. 'I locked the safe. No question about it.'

'Then why didn't you tell the police?'

'They said the alarm could have been triggered by an electrical surge. I didn't argue. It's best they believe that for the moment.'

Archie's brain was spinning. 'Is anything missing?'

'An artefact,' Rufus told him.

Cecille couldn't help herself. 'An artefact! Who would break into the bank to steal an *artefact*? Who would know it was there?' She said this as she took a packet of biscuits out of the cupboard and handed them to Jeffrey. They were too preoccupied to hear Rufus mutter, 'Not who, but *what*?'

But Archie heard.

Jeffrey went down to his study with his mug of tea and biscuits to make some phone calls regarding the bank 'incident', including a call to George's father, who was his assistant manager. Cecille went to put her new shoes upstairs and run a bath, which left Archie and Rufus sitting alone in the kitchen. Archie saw this as an opportunity, at long last, to talk to Rufus.

He got up from the table, went out into the hall to make sure they weren't being overheard, then sat down again. 'After I came back from fishing on Sunday you asked if I had swallowed any sea water.'

Rufus nodded.

'And I should tell you if I felt unusual?'

'Yes.'

'As well as static shocks, my fingers and toes keep tingling. A bit like when I was struck by lightning inside Huigor. I'm sure it happens when I'm close to curse activity.'

'Go on.'

'I keep hearing an army marching, and ever since a drip of water fell from the ceiling on to my spine I've been feeling . . .' He searched for the word that would best describe the sensation. 'Wired!' he decided.

Archie reached into his pocket, pulled out the pebble that was wrapped in paper and put it on the table. Then he handed the list to Rufus.

'I think you should read this.'

Rufus merely glanced at it before saying, 'All this since Sunday? Anything else?'

Archie was intrigued, since it implied Rufus expected

even more unusual occurrences. He pointed to the pebble wrapped in paper that was lying on the table.

'The gull on the window sill spat it out.'

'Can I take a look?'

'I haven't washed it yet,' Archie warned as Rufus removed the paper from the pebble and stared at it.

'It looks just like the one on my list,' Archie explained. 'The one I found on the shingle beach by the museum. I thought I'd seen the last of it after George threw it into the sea, but then it came rolling down the pavement out of the mist and stopped right at my feet. I think the same herring gull brought it back to me.'

Rufus looked at him. 'Mist?'

Archie nodded.

Rufus turned his attention back to the stone. 'Discovering that pebble on the beach was not a coincidence. It was deliberately placed there for you to find.'

'Why?'

'I'm not sure . . . yet. Can I see your pebble?'

Archie delved into his trouser pocket. He pulled out sweet papers, an elastic band, a blunt pencil sharpener and finally the green stone. He was careful to keep the gold key hidden in his pocket out of sight of Rufus.

Archie placed the pebble on the table. It was fractionally smaller than the other one and on closer inspection the carved arrow on the top was also smaller. But it was the stone the seagull had just brought to the window ledge that intrigued Rufus the most.

'Here's something else to add to your List of Unusual Occurrences,' he said. 'This is the missing artefact from my safe deposit box.'

Chapter Seventeen

Rufus was staring at the pebble as though he half expected it to explain how it had come to be in the gull's beak.

Archie was trying to make sense of the bizarre situation. 'Why would anyone want to steal a pebble?' he asked. 'Is it valuable?'

'It's priceless,' Rufus told him. 'There are only four in the world and we have two of them right here.'

'Where did you find the one that was in your safe deposit box?' Archie asked.

'I found it at the top of Ork Hill the night you broke the Stringweed curse,' Rufus told him. 'I was checking Monika for damage and the pebble was lodged inside a large clump of heather caught around one wheel. It had been spinning inside Huigor for hundreds of years. Now something wants it back.'

'Why?'

'It is foretold in I.C.E.'s ancient archives that when

all four pebbles come together curse activity will be destroyed for ever.'

Archie was intrigued. 'Do you know where the other two pebbles are?'

'Nobody knows. And if it hadn't been for the gull we might have lost this one tonight. I can only assume the gull snatched the pebble away from whatever took it out of the bank. What I am sure of, is that whatever opened the safe wasn't human. It got into the bank by walking through solid walls and doors and was able to open the safe without a key.'

Archie gasped. 'The ghost of Captain Bloodeye!'

Rufus managed a smile. 'You're forgetting one thing. A pebble is solid. It can't travel through walls and doors. It was brought out some other way . . . But how?'

They would have continued staring at the pebble, but a shrill scream sounded upstairs. Everyone seemed to be moving at once. Rufus put his pebble in his pocket, Archie grabbed his one too and they dashed out into the hall, almost colliding with Jeffrey, who had come running up from the basement. He led the way up the stairs to find Cecille standing on the landing in her bathrobe, shaking and pointing into the bathroom.

'Face . . . at the window.'

'Cecille, we're on the first floor!' Jeffrey told her.

Rufus was already in the bathroom and sticking his

head out the window. They could hear next door's dog barking and growling. Rufus pulled his head back in and shook the rain from his hair.

'There's nothing out there. Are you sure you saw a face?'

Cecille was quite sure. 'Yes! It had red eyes!'

Rufus stopped brushing the rain from his hair and stared at her. 'Red eyes?'

'Could it have been a bird?' Jeffrey suggested. 'After all, the window was steamed up . . .'

Cecille shook her head. 'No. Too big.' Her nervous expression quickly changed when she noticed Archie staring at her. She tried to make light of the situation by saying, 'Probably just my imagination,' yet she couldn't bring herself to have a bath.

They all gathered in the kitchen and Archie made a pot of tea and put a plateful of biscuits on the table, which nobody ate. Nobody was talking either. It was up to next door's dog and its constant barking to break the uneasy silence. Rufus sat staring thoughtfully into his mug.

Eventually, Cecille asked Jeffrey if pest control had caught the rat inside the bank and he replied, 'No, but they found a small hole down in the strongroom. That must be how it got inside the building.'

The dog stopped barking and Rufus stood up and announced, 'I have to go out.'

'Can I come out with you?' Archie asked.

Cecille quickly intervened, reminding him of the I.C.E. presentation the following evening in Edinburgh. 'Two late nights midweek isn't a good idea.'

Archie thought about protesting but to his disappointment Rufus announced he wanted to go out alone.

Jeffrey took one look at the rain running down the kitchen window. 'Take the Land Rover. It's too wet to go out on the bike.'

He pulled the keys from his pocket and when he came to place them in Rufus's hand he saw it was trembling. Cecille noticed it too.

Once Rufus had put his coat on and they heard the front door close, Cecille looked at Jeffrey as if to say, 'I told you. Rufus is ill.'

But Jeffrey was otherwise distracted. He was standing at the window and looking out into the night. 'I wonder what was making the dog bark.'

Archie was up in his room looking at the weatherscope. The planets were making tiny see-saw vibrations, much like the flutter of excitement he felt each time he thought about visiting the I.C.E. headquarters.

He reached under his bed for the box of artefacts and pulled out his medals, which he set down on his bedside table, ready for the morning. 'This time tomorrow night,' he assured himself, 'I will know for sure what is going on.'

This quelled his disappointment at not going out with Rufus but he couldn't suppress a yawn. He put the green pebble under his pillow for safe keeping and wondered where in the world the other two pebbles might be. Then he yawned again.

All the thoughts buzzing around in his head were making him tired and he fell asleep to the sound of the grandfather clock chiming eleven o'clock, reminding him that Rufus was still not home.

Chapter Eighteen

Rufus parked the Land Rover at the end of a grassy track above the beach, wound the window down just far enough to allow the chilly air to drift in and then he sat watching the rain on the windows. He was thinking about the trip he had just made to the top of Ork Hill.

It was the first time he had been up there since the night Archie had broken the Stringweed family curse, and what he'd seen disturbed him. The light from his torch had shown quite clearly a large circle of flattened and scorched earth around the Second World War memorial where the Stringweed curse had been exterminated. He had also found fresh scars on the ground: narrow channels that had been carved by something that moved. He had followed these unusual tracks until they came to the banks of an overflowing stream. Something that had survived the extermination had used the stream to carry it down the hillside. But to where? And why?

Archie's List of Unusual Occurrences, together with I.C.E. research, indicated this curse activity was becoming more complex by the day, and now inhuman hands had removed the pebble from his safe deposit box.

Rufus hoped the visit to the I.C.E. headquarters the following evening would shed new light on the situation. In the meantime he was going to have to be extra vigilant. He reached up and touched the raw scar on the back of his neck – the result of last night's attack outside Windy Edge.

It had happened when he had just got back from the Point and was locking up the Land Rover. Without warning a large creature had leapt on to his back and he'd felt its mouth searching for a place to bite his neck. Fortunately the collar of his flying jacket was turned up and he was wearing his hat. His gloves, too, had protected his hands as he struggled to throw the animal off, but it wasn't until he saw his reflection in the Land Rover wing mirror that he had seen, to his horror, a pair of red eyes peering over his shoulder.

If it hadn't been for next door's dog jumping over the garden gate and startling the creature away, Rufus suspected he would have sustained a more serious injury. He had managed to catch only a brief glimpse of the creature as it disappeared into the night, too brief to be sure of its shape, but he had seen red eyes like that only once before.

Was it possible that Monstrum, his deadliest enemy, was back? In which case was this strange new energy capable of awakening dead curses?

Rufus closed the Land Rover window. There was a distinct change in the air. It felt heavy and foreboding and was filled with the stench of rotting fish. He had come across this particular smell before during his travels and he recognised it as the odour of water-based curse activity. He picked up a large torch and jumped out of the car.

'OK. Let's go,' he said and the black Labrador that lived in the house next to Windy Edge leapt out. 'Keep your eyes and ears open,' Rufus told it. 'You know what to look for.'

Together they walked down to the beach with the roar of the sea in their ears and the moon casting occasional light upon the wet sand. They came upon the carcass of a seal, its body cleaned of flesh, and rocks covered in a green slime that stretched all the way to the caves.

Once there, Rufus shone the torch on to a heavy nail hammered into the cliff face. Hanging from it was a length of strong wire that reached down into the sea. He pulled up the wire and the Labrador whined excitedly as a can emerged out of the water. Rufus unhooked the can, set it down next to a rock pool and opened it. A pair of small glassy eyes appeared out of a clump of seaweed, and without warning two thin creamy tentacles shot out and wrapped themselves around his wrist.

Rufus grabbed the tentacles and pulled a Jellat out of the can. As it dangled from his gloved hand it gave a high-pitched wail, and less than a minute later it was dead and decaying.

'Interesting,' he said as he threw the stinking slimy mess back into the sea.

The dog turned towards the caves and gave a warning bark.

'What is it?' Rufus asked and the dog barked again.

Rufus shone his torch into the cave entrance and found himself looking at a swirling mass of water that looked as if it was being stirred by a giant spoon. Inside this surge of water were tentacles and flickering yellow lights.

'Run!' Rufus warned and he and the dog hurried away over the slippery rocks towards higher ground. Behind them, the water came roaring out of the cave and Rufus looked back to see the swell carrying Jellats out to sea.

He heard a squawk beside him and the herring gull came in to land.

'You know something, don't you?' Rufus asked it.

And the gull squawked, 'Yes.'

Chapter Nineteen

Back at Windy Edge, Archie had woken up from a restless sleep and was now wide awake. He got out of bed and looked through the window to the empty space outside the gate where the Land Rover usually stood.

Minutes later, he was sitting at the bottom of the stairs slipping his feet into damp shoes. The time on the grandfather clock was just after one o'clock in the morning. He had pulled his clothes on over his pyjamas and he zipped his jacket up as he walked through the kitchen into the back hallway. He wheeled his bike out into the rainy night and pulled up his hood and when he was beyond the gate he swung his leg over the crossbar and set off at speed down the hill. As he approached Ezekiel's house, he took a sharp right and pedalled as fast as he could. His intended destination was the Point and he was going to find out for himself what Rufus was doing there.

His determination faltered a little when he approached the village outskirts. Beyond the brightly lit speed limit signs the road was dark and empty, but he persevered, as would be expected of an I.C.E. medal holder. However he couldn't help a shiver of nervousness as he sped by the gates of ghostly Ormleigh House with only the glow from his bike light to show him the way.

It had stopped raining by the time he reached the beach, but the air felt heavy as he cycled along the hard wet sand. He found it difficult to breathe and there was a peculiar stench, like rotten fish.

The tide was out, but a strong swell was running, and though cloud covered the moon he could see that the water along the shoreline was sparkling. He left his bike on the sand and walked towards the water's edge to take a closer look at the mesmerising lights. As he watched, they began to go in and out of focus. He rubbed his eyes and suddenly felt very sleepy, too sleepy to bother moving his feet, which were sinking into the soft sand. He liked the sensation. It resembled a big comfortable bed inviting him to lie down and let the waves roll over him like a heavy quilt. He wanted to curl up and fall asleep to the sound of high-pitched wailing that was coming at him from all directions. Yet something was keeping him awake. A persistent rhythm was growing steadily louder in his ears, until it drowned out the wailing and Archie was roused from his stupor by the sound of an army on the march.

He blinked himself awake. The flickering lights had disappeared, the wailing had fallen silent, but the sound of an advancing army continued to close in. Archie turned and ran back up the beach to where he had left his bike. He picked it up and glanced back over his shoulder towards the sea. A shallow layer of black water had separated from the rolling waves and was advancing up the sand at a speed that showed no sign of ebbing.

The moon appeared from behind a cloud and he saw it wasn't a layer of water at all but thousands of crabs emerging out of the sea in horseshoe formation. The crabs at the front were the size of soup plates, while those at the back were as big as black umbrellas, and those were just the ones he could see.

He began to run but the wet sand and the bike slowed him down. With the claws already snapping close to his heels he dropped the bike and took a running leap on to a cluster of rocks. But as he made for the safety of the headland the ground beneath him moved. He looked down to see he was standing on the back of a gigantic crab, and he gave a surprised yelp. He jumped on to another rock but that moved too, as did the next and the next, because the headland was now a heaving mass of crabs.

Gigantic pincers grabbed Archie's legs and passed

him from claw to claw. He was terrified, yet reassured by their gentle hold on him as he was set down on the sand beside his bike. Immediately, the sound of marching stopped and the beach fell silent. He was too terrified to move.

Six gigantic crabs broke through the ranks to tower over him, waving their pincers and clashing them together like swords. Were they about to cut his arms off? Was he to be eaten alive?

Archie wasn't prepared for what happened next. The smaller crabs scuttled aside to clear a path that led to the top of the beach. As Archie cautiously picked up his bike and pushed it along the newly created path, he was aware of large waving claws either side of him.

He was breathless and shaking by the time he dragged the bike up over the boulders on to the grassy track above the beach. But there before him was the parked Land Rover. Empty and locked. Archie managed to stop shaking long enough to get the gold key out of his pocket, let himself in and pull the door shut.

Then he stared out through the windscreen into the darkness. He could hear nothing other than the distant roar of the sea and the occasional drop of rain on the windscreen. There was no sound of a marching army. Were the crabs still gathered on the Point? Tonight they had saved him from the Jellats and directed him towards the protection of the Land Rover. But why?

Chapter Twenty

Rufus found Archie curled up on the passenger seat of the Land Rover. His eyes were wide and his voice shook as he said, 'There's an army of gigantic crabs out there. That's the sound of marching I've been hearing! Shut the door!'

But Rufus opened it wider and Archie gave a nervous yelp as the Labrador clambered in and settled itself on the back seat.

'What's he doing here?' Archie asked as the dog panted and drooled close to his ear.

'He fancied a walk.'

Archie thought Rufus seemed unnaturally calm. He appeared in no hurry to attach the bike to the car roof, get into the Land Rover and start the engine. Only after the windscreen had been cleared of greenish dirt did he turn to Archie and ask, 'What are you doing out here?'

Archie chose his words carefully. 'I was looking for you.'

'Why?'

'I need to know what's going on.'

'Not even I.C.E. fully knows what's going on. I told you to wait for instructions and not take things into your own hands.'

'But if I'm to break the curse –'

'There's no guarantee you're suited to breaking this curse. Even if you are, I.C.E. has a Code of Practice. Exterminators have to be invited to break a curse. You still have a lot to learn. Tonight you found yourself in a very dangerous situation with no one to help. If you take things into your hands again, you may risk someone else's life as well as your own.'

Archie was about to apologise but Rufus was still talking. 'Luckily for you the Glimpers came ashore tonight.'

'Glimpers?'

Rufus put the Land Rover in gear and they set off along the track.

'Do you remember the news report with Slaverin' Joe?'

'Yes.'

'The crabs that were caught in the fishing nets are called Glimpers. The shadow I saw in the sea near Moss Rock was them on the move. They travel along the seabed during daylight. Just before sunset they rise towards the surface. At night they fold their legs beneath their bodies and surf the waves. They have small air pockets on the underside of their bodies to keep them afloat.'

'I've heard them marching down at the harbour and through the kitchen sink at Windy Edge as well.'

Rufus didn't appear too surprised. 'They hibernate on the seabed until awakened by curse activity. Their purpose is to destroy the Jellats. It was a Glimper that delivered the pebble to the beach. Focus on the sound they emit and it will break the Jellats' hold over you.'

'How do you know a Glimper brought me the pebble?'

'The herring gull told me. It had to retrieve the pebble when George threw it back into the water.'

Archie was trying to keep up with the increasingly bizarre revelations. 'You had a conversation with a gull?'

'Not exactly a conversation. They have a limited vocabulary. I asked questions and it gave either a "yes" or "no" answer.'

'Looks like I missed all the fun.'

'Sitting in the cold for hours monitoring unusual marine activity is not fun. Curse extermination isn't just about using the artefacts. It also involves painstaking research and patience.'

Something occurred to Archie. 'Aren't you affected by the Jellats' wailing?'

'No. Not everyone can hear the high pitch. Those

who do find themselves being drawn towards the Jellats.'

They had just passed the entrance to Ormleigh Lodge and were fast approaching the crossroads when the dog started to bark. Rufus put his foot down hard on the accelerator.

'Must have seen a rabbit.'

The dog continued to bark until they sped past the village speed signs. Then it turned and sat staring out through the rear windows until they reached Windy Edge.

Rufus got out first and lifted the bike down from the car roof. Archie was careful not to slam the car door. They didn't talk as they walked around the house to the back door, and while Rufus rewarded the Labrador with a packet of chocolate buttons, Archie was already tiptoeing up the attic stairs. He was too tired to think any more about curse activity or the magnificent army of Glimpers or the talking herring gull. It would wait until morning. He threw off his jacket and jeans and crawled into bed, and his eyes were closed by the time he pulled the quilt up to his chin. Even so a last sleepy thought drifted through his mind. If there was no guarantee he would be invited to battle this curse activity, why then had the Glimper specially delivered the pebble to him?'

Chapter Twenty-one

Overnight, a strange melancholy had descended across Westervoe. The roads and the main street were almost empty at 8 a.m. when people would normally be making their way to work. Grey clouds hung low in the sky and rain dripped from window sills and doorways to gather in deep puddles.

Archie's teacher, Mr Taylor, who was always showered and dressed by 7.30 a.m., didn't open his eyes until 8.03 and it was 8.21 a.m. before he crawled out of bed. His head ached, his eyes burned and his skin felt as if it was crawling with lice. He put this down to restless dreams about his grandfather, who had drowned in a trench during the First World War.

A similar situation was developing at Slaverin' Joe's house. He had wakened to a feeling of tightness around his throat that made it difficult to swallow. When he looked in the bathroom mirror, he discovered a red mark all the way round his neck. There was a sinister addition to this scenario. He too had woken from disturbing dreams about an ancestor: a woman who had been condemned as a witch and hanged at the gallows.

But it wasn't just bad dreams affecting people. Mr Ashburn, the baker, was surveying the black and green mould covering his entire stock of flour. Already he owed the bank more money than he could pay and he was trying hard not to think of his Great Uncle Willie, who had died destitute on the streets of Glasgow.

All along the waterfront, homes that had been warm and dry the night before felt cold and damp. Strange fungi had appeared on ceilings close to water pipes, moss was growing along even the most carefully tended paths, and windows were coated in a film of green grime that even the heavy rain couldn't wash away.

All across Westervoe, behind closed doors and drawn curtains, people were waking up to find that things were not as they had been the night before.

Chapter Twenty-two

When Archie walked into the school cloakroom that morning, he overheard Sid talking with two younger boys.

'. . . *and* there were two rats outside the bakery –'

'That's nothing!' one of the boys interrupted. 'Our garden path is covered in worms. Hundreds of them!'

'Where do you think the smell in the air is coming from?' the other boy asked. 'It's like rotten eggs,' he gasped, before launching into a chesty cough.

Sid noticed Archie. He walked over to where he was hanging up his coat.

'Hardly anybody's at school today,' he told Archie. 'I think the damp weather's got something to do with it. My brother's back on his inhaler.'

Sid's trousers had a wet band on each leg where his coat didn't quite reach the top of his wellies, and a drip of green mucus was hanging from one of his nostrils. He shuffled closer to Archie and in a conspiratorial voice said, 'I found out something about Ruby.'

Archie was suddenly a lot more interested in what Sid had to say. 'What about Ruby?' he asked.

Sid's eyes sparkled with intrigue. 'When I went back to the classroom yesterday to get George's worksheet, I heard Mrs Merriman say to Mr Taylor –'

'What are you two talking about?' asked a grumpy voice.

They turned to see George pulling down his wet hood. His eyes were puffy and he had an ugly cold sore on his upper lip.

'We're not talking about anything,' Sid told him.

George dropped his rucksack to the floor. 'Keep your secret. I don't care.' Then, ignoring Sid, he turned to Archie. 'Who do you think broke into the bank last night?'

Sid looked at Archie. 'There was a bank robbery? Did they get any money? Did they catch them?' His eyes had the wide look of someone both excited and scared.

George ignored Sid's questions and carried on talking. 'Some people say it was your Uncle Rufus trying to break in.'

Archie couldn't hide his irritation. 'Don't be daft. He was with us when the police phoned.'

George shrugged. 'I'm only saying what other people are saying.'

'What are they saying?' Archie asked.

'That he was in the strongroom yesterday afternoon and how come he can afford to fly an aeroplane when he doesn't work.'

'He does work!' said Archie.

'Doing what?'

Because Archie couldn't admit Rufus was a curse exterminator he said, 'He's an explorer.'

George laughed cruelly. 'Not much call for an explorer in Westervoe!'

Sid jumped to Archie's defence. 'You think you know everything, George Ratteray. Well, I know something you don't.'

At that moment the door to the cloakroom swung open and Ruby walked in. Sid immediately stopped arguing and proceeded to watch Ruby hang up her wet coat. Once or twice he glanced across to Archie, making George suspect their secret had something to do with her. Perhaps Ruby sensed the tension too, because she rested her eyes on the three boys in turn while slipping on her indoor shoes. But whatever thoughts were going through her head were for her alone. She stood up, and before strolling out the door she made a point of smiling at Archie and wishing him 'Good morning', which infuriated George all the more.

Sid, meantime, was quietly considering the information he had learned about Ruby.

* * *

Mr Taylor was standing guard outside the classroom door preventing anyone from entering. There was an egg stain on his tie. His hair looked as if it needed a wash and he was slouched against the door frame as though he couldn't be bothered to stand up.

'What's going on?' Archie asked the one person who was sure to know.

'There's an alien in there!' Linda told him. 'I heard Mrs Merriman talking to Mr Petrie. She said, "It's not of this world!"'

Mr Petrie, the janitor, came striding down the corridor wearing a makeshift apron made from a green bin liner and waving a mop and bucket. 'Make way. Make way.'

Mr Taylor opened the classroom door and Archie jostled with the rest of the class to get a look inside. One or two children gasped.

Up on the ceiling, next to the window and above the fish tank, was a fungus the size of an enormous pumpkin, except it was blue and purple and yellow.

Suzie wrinkled her nose. 'It smells of rotten fish.'

Mr Petrie began to prod the fungus with the mop handle. 'You say it just appeared overnight?'

But Mr Taylor was in no mood for chit-chat. 'We can't just leave it there. There must be something you can do.'

Mr Petrie lowered the mop and announced, 'This is a job for Environmental Health.'

The area beneath the fungus was cordoned off with chairs from the staffroom, and the door was kept open to allow the air to circulate.

During all this commotion Archie had been waiting for an opportunity to look inside the art cupboard for the shadow. Was it even still in there? He found it difficult to concentrate on anything else except maybe Ruby. Her behaviour that day was certainly strange. He'd seen her slip a handful of fish food into her trouser pocket and each time she walked by the tank the fish would dart behind a log. What was it Sid had found out about her? He wished he could find an opportunity to ask him without being overheard by George, who was keeping a close eye on both of them.

By mid-morning Suzie and Sid both complained that the odour was making them feel sick and their parents were called to take them home.

By lunchtime there were more complaints of sore throats, itchy eyes and, bizarrely, two pupils discovered verrucas on their feet when changing for PE.

The official from Environmental Health arrived, took one look at the fungus and announced, 'Westervoe is in the grip of a fungi epidemic.'

Later that afternoon a rat was seen in the canteen, fungi were discovered in the toilets and, when a strong odour began to permeate the building, it was decided to close the school for the rest of the week in order to carry out a full investigation.

The school secretary handed out letters of explanation to parents, and Mr Petrie placed an extra-large fan heater in the classroom to dry out the fungus.

Archie, meantime, was looking at the wall clock with a creeping excitement. Straight after school he was setting off for the I.C.E. headquarters in Edinburgh. Even the information Sid knew about Ruby was temporarily forgotten when at long last Mr Petrie rang the 3.30 p.m. bell at 3.33.

Chapter Twenty-three

Just as Jeffrey had suspected, the drive to Edinburgh was slow and hazardous. His eyes were screwed up the entire journey as he struggled to see through the rain-lashed windscreen.

By the time they crawled into the city centre, stopped twice to ask directions (Jeffrey had forgotten the invitation with the map on the back) and finally parked close to the castle, they weren't in a party mood.

Cecille's hair was so frizzy it looked as if it had been washed in lemonade and conditioned with candyfloss. She tried salvaging her appearance by applying a swipe of lipstick and spraying on some perfume. Jeffrey stretched the tension out of his neck and took a fresh tie from his jacket pocket. 'Ready?' he asked, and they all jumped out in a coordinated swoop, slammed the doors shut and ran through the rain towards a short flight of steps leading to a recessed doorway.

A single nameplate read 'Carthusian Historical

Society' and it was so highly polished Archie could see his rain-speckled reflection in it. They were ringing the doorbell when someone dressed head to toe in blue waterproofs and wearing a motorcycle helmet walked out carrying a bundle of envelopes.

Archie grabbed the door before it closed and they all walked into an empty hallway that was completely silent but for the click of the door shutting behind them.

A small chandelier hung from a high ceiling, lighting up the mustard-coloured walls and yellowing paint-work. Up ahead a staircase twisted out of sight towards the first floor and beneath it was a flight of stone steps leading down to the basement.

'Do you think we're at the right place?' Cecille whispered.

Footsteps sounded on the staircase and they looked up to see a tall man in a tweed suit descend from the first floor. He pushed long strands of white hair back from his brow and smiled politely.

'Mr and Mrs Stringweed, I presume. And Archie?'

Cecille suddenly appeared nervous. She brushed creases from her coat and discreetly wiped her front teeth with her tongue as the man walked towards them with his hand extended. 'A pleasure to meet you all.'

He shook each of their hands in turn and introduced himself as Professor Neville Himes.

The group spent a minute or two on such pleasantries as the difficulty of their journey, how pleased they were with the family tree Cecille had commissioned Professor Himes to trace for her just before Christmas, and how she really should get round to ordering some more. When all these niceties were out of the way, Professor Himes smiled and said, 'Come and meet an important member of the I.C.E. team.'

Archie was the first to follow Professor Himes down the narrow stone steps leading to the basement. The rush of rainwater through the drainpipes gave the impression of being inside a warm cave, and the ceiling was so low you had to tilt your head at the bottom to avoid hitting an overhang from which hung a single light bulb. The overall feel was old but clean, with whitewashed walls which were covered in framed black and white photographs of very serious-looking men and women.

Up ahead a hoarse voice could be heard asking, 'Who goes there?'

Archie was still trying to tell if it was a man or a woman who had spoken when the voice broke off and there was a rapid series of sneezes.

'Miss Napier?' Professor Himes said to the invisible person. 'We have guests.'

They followed him along the narrow corridor, passing five or six small rooms. Through the open doors these rooms resembled a library, but upon closer inspection Archie noticed the shelves contained not books but rolled-up cream parchment paper tied with either a yellow, blue, green or red ribbon.

From behind one of the floor-to-ceiling bookcases a woman appeared, flicking crumbs from the front of her brown cardigan.

'Ah, Miss Napier,' Professor Himes was now saying. 'Our guests have arrived.'

Miss Napier was small and her grey hair was pulled into a knot at the back of her head with occasional tired wisps hanging unintentionally over her ears. The back of her neck was lost somewhere inside the thick collar of her cardigan. She looked at them over the top of her glasses which were attached to a gold chain around her neck. She wore a curious yet good-natured expression.

'Who do we have here?' she asked, licking the remainder of the crumbs from her lips.

'Let me introduce the Stringweed family,' said Professor Himes.

Miss Napier removed her glasses and exchanged them for a second pair. She poked her head forward like a tortoise peering out of its shell and Archie detected the scent of sugar.

Professor Himes continued his introductions, pointing to each individual as he spoke. 'Jeffrey, Cecille and Archie, I'd like to introduce Miss Eunice Napier.'

Miss Napier smiled. 'Well. This *is* an honour.' She shook hands first with Archie and then Jeffrey. She adjusted her glasses to look more closely at Cecille while shaking her hand. 'How are you?' she enquired.

'Fine, thank you.'

But Miss Napier wasn't satisfied with this reply. 'Sure?'

'Yes.'

'Any fainting spells, forgetfulness –'

Professor Himes gave a short cough. 'Miss Napier is our Keeper of the Codicils. And a very fine job she does too. One of our most experienced employees.'

'Thirty-five years next month,' she said proudly.

'Congratulations,' Jeffrey felt obliged to say. 'I hope you're in a good pension scheme.'

'Keeper of the Codicils?' said Cecille thoughtfully. 'Aren't codicils legal documents? Amendments to a will?'

Miss Napier shrugged and almost disappeared inside the cardigan collar. 'The legal profession stole the term from us. But having the same name is useful. We find it confuses unauthorised persons who find their way down here. They soon lose interest in thousands of legal documents.'

'And as Keeper of the Codicils, what exactly is it you do?' Cecille went on to ask.

Miss Napier gave a flattered smile. 'If you'd care to

follow me,' she said, 'I shall explain as best I can.'

They followed her to the end of the corridor and into a room with a sign above the open doorway saying 'Map Room'. With a flourish of her hand she waved at shelves upon shelves of rolled parchment.

'As Keeper of the Codicils, it is my responsibility to track curses. As each curse is traced, it is named, dated and logged on parchment and then filed under one of the four elements . . . earth, water, fire and air, sub-filed alphabetically, then cross-referenced under active or inactive.'

They weaved their way through the shelves until they came upon a big circular wooden table. Spread upon it was a large round map of the world. It was old and yellowing and showed in detail the position of mountain ranges, rivers, lakes, oceans and coastlines.

Miss Napier took a deep breath and pointed to the map. 'Countries, cities, towns, they come and go. Our real interest is the geography of the world.' She pointed to a series of coloured pins on the map, some of which had small labels attached. 'The pins indicate the position and path of curses that I'm currently tracking. You see, curses use the Earth's magnetism to travel.'

'Fascinating,' said Jeffrey, who was looking at a large cluster of green pins around the Baltic region. He noticed one or two close to Westervoe as well.

'Some curses jog along without creating too much

havoc,' Miss Napier explained. 'They have no serious intent. A grudge really, rather than a curse. An outbreak of boils, for instance, a persistent cough, an itchy rash, indoor plants that keep dying, losing keys, that kind of thing. They're Grade 1 and 2. Then there's Grade 3. Bit more of a nuisance, but still too lightweight to spend time tracking, unless we get a specific request. It's really Grades 4, 5 and 6 we monitor closely.'

'What do these grades do?' Archie asked.

'Grade 4 can inflict physical symptoms, including prolonged headaches, visual disturbance and nausea. It also affects atmospheric conditions, such as heavy mist, static. Grade 5 is responsible for severe weather patterns.' She gave Archie a knowing look. 'Tornadoes, for example. Grade 5 also affects the human condition to a far greater extent. It produces dissatisfaction, quite often leading to civil unrest. Grade 6 is an extreme case of Grade 5 and it is at this level we often see the outbreak of war. It calls for fastidious monitoring.'

Archie was fascinated. 'How do you monitor curses, Miss Napier?'

'Aaah! Interesting question. Curses cannot be electronically monitored,' she informed him. 'Curse tracking is a delicate and erratic process. It requires a very specific kind of talent. It cannot be learned. Humans who have the ability inherit it. Creatures of high intelligence have been known to feel the force, too. Elephants are particularly susceptible, as well as dolphins, dogs and pigs.'

'Is it just curse activity you can sense?' Cecille enquired. 'What about sixth sense? Can you see ghosts, for instance?'

Professor Himes intervened at this point. He stepped forward and with an outstretched arm gently guided Cecille towards the basement steps.

'I'm sure you could all do with some refreshments after your journey. I'll show you to the reception room on the first floor.'

Archie wasn't interested in refreshments, and when Miss Napier invited him to stay and chat a little longer he readily accepted. When they were alone, he asked her if the Stringweed curse had been logged on parchment paper.

'Of course!' she said, looking surprised that he should ask. 'It was a Grade 5. A very strong curse indeed. Gave me the most dreadful week-long headache.'

'Can I see the Stringweed curse codicil?'

Miss Napier appeared uncomfortable at his request. 'The codicil is not to hand at the moment . . . got one or two details to add. However . . .' She turned and climbed up a small set of wooden steps and selected a codicil from a high shelf. 'This one here is interesting. Dates back to 1923. A whole tribe in Zambia struck down with a most curious skin infection. A happy outcome thanks to one of our curse exterminators being in the area . . .'

'Do you know all the curses in these codicils?' Archie asked, looking around at the tightly packed shelves.

'Well . . . I wouldn't say *all* of them. Some are so old as to be obscure. But I have a good memory and a very good filing system.'

'So you could find any curse? If you had to?'

Miss Napier blinked heavily. 'Was there one in particular you were thinking of?'

Archie nodded. 'A cursed lion. In a jungle. It killed somebody.'

Miss Napier looked thoughtful. 'Nothing comes immediately to mind.' She was still considering this when they both heard a light tapping sound followed by a louder plop coming from the other side of the room.

'Oh no. Not *another* leak!'

'I've got a leak in my bedroom ceiling,' Archie told her. 'The rainwater is coloured. Why do you think that is?'

Miss Napier put her hand to her chest and gasped with excitement. 'Coloured rain, you say? Have you noticed a small wispy cloud at all, above the roof and close to the source of the leak?'

Archie nodded and Miss Napier gasped again. 'Icegull breath!' She turned serious. 'What are you collecting it in?'

'A bucket.'

'Metal?'

'Yes.'

'Marvellous.' She gave a loud sigh of relief and muttered, 'Just when I was running out.' She peered at him over the top of her glasses. 'Under no circumstances throw that rainwater out. I want you to check the water regularly. When you can see the colour of your eyes reflected in it you have mature Icegull breath.'

'Is that good news?'

'Good? It's marvellous! Icegull breath is the best ink in the world for writing up codicils.'

She gave another happy sigh, but a loud plop reminded her of the leak at the other side of the room and she quickly clattered down the stepladder. She then showed surprising strength by picking up the steps and carrying them to a corner of the room where a steady flow of water was dripping on to a shelf of codicils. She set the steps down next to a window that, bizarrely, had a blind hanging on the outside of it rather than the inside. Archie was figuring out why that might be when a box of doughnuts was thrust into his hands.

'I need to clear this table,' Miss Napier was saying as she brushed crumbs on to the floor.

Archie felt he should be doing something rather than just holding a box of doughnuts. 'Will I start clearing the shelf?' he asked.

'No!'

Miss Napier had spoken so loudly that Archie almost dropped the box of doughnuts. She leaned close to his face so that he could see fingerprints on her spectacles.

'Never, ever, ever handle the codicils without my consent. You'll change their energy. No one can handle the codicils except me. Do you understand?'

Her expression was so serious that Archie immediately told her he understood.

Her voice softened again. 'In the world of I.C.E., nothing is ever what it seems, Archie. Always expect the unexpected.'

Meanwhile the water was continuing to drip on to the shelf.

'Maybe I should go and find a pot or something?' he said as a secondary leak appeared.

Miss Napier agreed. 'Good idea. Get two or three!"

There were no pots to be seen, but he did find a large floral teacup and an empty inkwell that he thought would do until he found something larger. He positioned them carefully on the shelf.

Miss Napier continued to stack the damp codicils on the marble-topped table, stopping occasionally to wipe a line of sweat from her top lip. Her nose had begun to twitch and she sneezed violently while searching the right-hand pocket of her skirt. She pulled out a lace handkerchief and a small bottle made of dark blue glass that looked like an old-fashioned perfume bottle except that it had a small lever protruding from the neck. She inserted the tip of the bottle into a nostril and began pumping the lever with her thumb. Archie could hear the hiss of fine liquid being sprayed into her nose. She sniffed twice and announced, 'Aah! That's better. There's a lot of negative energy around at the moment,' she explained. 'Makes me very congested.'

'My nose gets itchy too,' Archie told her. 'I'm allergic to fur and hair. That's why I can't have a cat or dog.'

Miss Napier opened the box of mini jam doughnuts and offered it to him. He remembered his manners and took just the one.

Miss Napier returned to the subject of her congestion. 'The cause of my itch is rather more complicated than the presence of cats or dogs. You see, Archie, you have to think of my head as the world.' She pointed to a small mole between her eyebrows. 'In which case we're here.' She pulled her right ear lobe. 'This is New York and this here . . .' She pulled her left ear. 'This is Moscow.' She laid her palm across the top of her head. 'Strong magnetic pulls in the North give me a headache while those in the South produce a sore throat. Strong curse activity in Indonesia can quite literally be a pain in the neck.'

A drop of water bounced out of the floral cup and landed on the shelf with a plop. Miss Napier busied herself with the job of moving yet more codicils away from the spreading puddle and Archie went in search of a larger vessel. As he began climbing the basement stairs, he heard her urge, 'Quickly now! Strong curse activity on the move,' and then she sneezed again.

Chapter Twenty-four

Archie ran all the way up to the first floor. He could hear the clink of china and the sound of voices and he could hear a woman's high-pitched laugh.

He made his way along the corridor towards the source of the laughter and stopped at the open doorway of a high-ceilinged room. The walls were painted pale blue and directly opposite to where he stood was a large ornate mirror hanging above a marble fireplace. He flattened a tuft of hair sticking out above his right ear and took a look around the room.

Rufus had arrived. He was standing by a floor-to-ceiling window and talking earnestly with Professor Himes. Occasionally they'd look out into the heavy rain that made the city lights beyond the window look like wet paint running down glass. It crossed Archie's mind to walk over and say hello, but they appeared too deep in conversation to be disturbed. Instead he crossed the creaky wooden floor towards a group of people gathered around a long table covered with a white cloth. On this table stood three large teapots, cups, saucers, and plates of sandwiches and cakes. The sight of this food reminded Archie that all he'd had to eat since lunchtime was a bag of crisps in the car and one of Miss Napier's mini doughnuts. He began to examine the sandwich fillings and discovered they were all fish paste.

'Nice spread,' a man was telling Cecille. She gave a polite smile and the man continued talking. 'Glad to see they pulled out all the stops for the presentation.'

Cecille simply nodded because the man never stopped talking long enough to give her an opportunity to say anything. He was short and wore a garish black and white dog-tooth jacket. His large handlebar moustache wiggled as he talked and talked and talked.

'Yes . . . I recall 1968 was another bad year.' He gave a soft whistle. 'Protests, floods and an explosion in the rabbit population. Actually, I'm working on the grey squirrel/red squirrel dynamic at the moment . . .'

Jeffrey, on the other hand, was having a lively discussion with the woman who had the high-pitched laugh.

Archie put two fish paste sandwiches and three raisin fairy cakes on to a small plate, picked up an empty milk jug, which he thought would be a suitable vessel to catch drips, and returned to the basement.

Miss Napier had removed all the codicils from the

shelf and they were now stacked in a neat pyramid on the marble-topped table.

'I brought some sandwiches and cakes,' Archie told her.

She inspected the filling. 'Sardine paste!' She sighed wistfully. 'Oh, for some wild salmon terrine.' The mention of salmon seemed to trigger a thought. 'Do you like swimming?'

'I have trouble with my bilateral breathing,' he told her.

'Bilateral breathing?' She considered this for a moment. 'Breathing won't be a problem, but can you move like this?' She bent her legs at the knees and began to wave her arms in awkward frog-like circles.

Archie resisted the temptation to laugh. 'Yes, I can do that. Why?'

He didn't get a reply, because as quickly as the bizarre conversation had begun, it ended. Miss Napier's eyes were rolling around in their sockets.

'Energy!' she whispered, and a few more wisps of hair fell loose around her face.

She hurried over to the map table and exchanged her glasses for the second pair that hung on a chain around her neck. Then she began touching the glass-topped pins with the tips of her fingers. Her eyes were closed by now and she was humming to herself, except it wasn't a tune, just a single low note that sounded deep in her chest.

'Miss Napier?' Archie said softly.

She didn't respond. Her head was so close to the map that her nose was almost touching it. She kept one foot on the floor, and the other foot was raised slightly at the heel to keep her balance. Her body was swaying from side to side while she continued to hold that strange humming note. Archie could tell she was oblivious to everything but the curse energy she was now tracking. He was wondering how it felt to track curse energy when Miss Napier gave a loud moan and stood bolt upright. Her eyes were open and unblinking and she was so still that she hardly seemed to be breathing at all, yet there was a frantic squealing that sent shivers up his spine.

'Miss Napier?' he asked again, but she remained locked in her trance-like state.

Archie's eyes were searching the room, wondering what he should do and whether the squealing sound meant Miss Napier was in some kind of distress. He caught sight of a movement on the floor. A mouse was running on the spot, its tail trapped under the heel of Miss Napier's shoe. She was totally unaware of the squealing and the mouse's desperate attempts to scamper away, so Archie got down on his hands and knees and crawled over to the table while whispering words of comfort to the small creature, which was now rigid with fear. He was also quietly praying that Miss Napier wouldn't wake from her trance and find him there.

He placed his fingers around the heel of her shoe and was immediately blinded by a strong white flash. He heard a faint animalistic squeal, there was a grotesque smell of burning and then everything went black.

Chapter Twenty-five

When Archie regained consciousness, he found Miss Napier kneeling beside him. He could smell something sweet and sickly and he realised she was holding the blue glass bottle under his nose. His nostrils felt as if they were on fire and when he sat up everything began to spin. He groaned and held his head.

'How do you feel?' Miss Napier asked and Archie groaned again.

She took hold of his wrist and checked his pulse. 'No cause for alarm. Normal!'

Archie looked around and saw he was no longer in the map room. Black and white photographs of serious-looking men and women frowned down at him from the walls.

'How come I'm in the corridor?'

'Did you touch me when I was in a trance?' she asked.

He nodded his head and the photographs started to spin. 'I gripped the heel of your shoe,' he mumbled.

Miss Napier sighed. 'Still, it could have been worse. A lot worse. It's fortunate that I was realigning when it happened.'

'Realigning?'

'Coming out of a trance,' she explained. 'I was channelling a particularly strong energy, too. The force threw you out into the corridor. Fortunately, you weren't seriously injured. Which is more than we can say for the poor mouse.' A frazzled lump of fur lay on the floor close to Archie.

'Had to peel its tail from my shoe,' she said with a grimace.

Archie pulled himself up on to his feet. He could hear the sound of distant clapping. 'The presentation! I can't miss it.'

Miss Napier peered into his eyes. 'Are you quite sure you're well enough to walk?'

'Yes,' Archie told her. 'Are you coming?'

Miss Napier shook her head. 'Have to get back to the map. Energy surges. Strong too.' She looked into his eyes. 'If you're sure you're all right . . .?'

'I'm fine,' he told her, which wasn't strictly true. His legs felt wobbly and there was a loud ringing in his ears and he tingled all over.

Miss Napier, however, accepted that he was well

enough to attend the presentation and she wandered back to the map room, sneezing violently and inhaling from her blue glass bottle.

Archie climbed the basement stairs. When he reached the ground floor, coloured spots appeared in front of his eyes. He could still hear clapping, and because he was anxious not to miss the presentation he steadied himself by gripping the banister and began to climb the next flight of stairs. Halfway up he stopped and squeezed his eyes to try and clear the spots, almost colliding with someone coming down.

By the time he reached the reception room on the first floor, everyone was in the process of raising a full cup of tea and saying, 'To Jeffrey!'

Archie looked at his father, who was smiling in a slightly bemused way. In his hand was an opened white envelope.

Archie sidled up to Cecille. 'What's happening?'

Cecille seemed surprisingly unenthusiastic, considering how much she had been looking forward to the presentation. She pulled a small fish bone from between her teeth. 'Apparently, your father has just received a year's free subscription to *I.C.E. Quarterly* . . . in recognition of his part in breaking the Stringweed curse.' She looked across to Jeffrey, who was still wearing his bemused smile. 'I don't know why we had to come all the way to Edinburgh. They could have stuck it in the post.'

Jeffrey, however, appeared to be enjoying the attention. The small crowd was congratulating him and slapping him on the back. Cecille couldn't hide her disappointment. She had stopped trying to flatten her frizzy hair, and with all thoughts of tiaras and Jeffrey getting a knighthood gone she began tucking into another fish paste sandwich. Archie chose not to add to her disappointment by telling her about his blackout. After all, he felt fine now – more or less. The spots in front of his eyes were gone, and although there was a slight echo in his ears his hearing felt sharper.

Archie looked around the room. Rufus was nowhere to be seen and not one person in the chattering noisy group was attempting to talk to Archie. No one had congratulated him on breaking the Stringweed curse and no one had remarked on his medals, which he had worn specially. More disappointing still, no one had invited him to exterminate the Westervoe curse. He might as well have been invisible. If no one noticed he was there, then no one would notice he was gone.

He wandered back out into the corridor. There were two varnished wooden doors, both of which were closed. But it was the tall double doors at the far end of the corridor that interested him the most, and as an I.C.E. medal holder he felt he had earned the right to explore.

He decided he might as well take a quick look inside the other two rooms as well. With the coast clear he crossed to the door opposite and, finding it unlocked, slipped into the room. Luckily, there was no one inside. He told himself he would have to be more careful on entering the other two rooms, which he hoped were more interesting than the one he was now looking round.

Against one wall were six tables stacked with newspapers printed in various languages. On the wall opposite were four tables and each held a single coloured in-tray. The blue tray was labelled 'Water', the brown tray 'Earth', the red tray 'Fire' and the green tray 'Air'.

In the blue tray were newspaper cuttings relating to floods, high tides, torrential rain. There was a charred piece of cloth in the red tray, the green tray was empty and the brown tray held a single photograph of a diseased elm tree.

The walls of the room were covered with various charts and maps and colour photographs of strange-looking creatures, including a giant octopus with a single red eye. But he had seen enough. There were the other two rooms to investigate.

With the coast still clear he crossed the corridor again to the second door. He took a moment to put his ear against it to check for sounds from within, discovered it was also unlocked, opened it and took a look inside.

It was a large room with no windows, and it reminded him of a picture he had seen of a telephone exchange from the 1950s. Unimpressed, he shut the door again.

The third room was only a few metres away from where he stood. Close up, the tall double doors looked even more impressive, as did the ornate brass doorknobs. He felt sure this room contained something important and he wasn't too surprised to find the doors locked. He put his hand in his pocket and took out the gold key. He looked over his shoulder to make sure he was still alone, unlocked the door and gently pushed it open.

He got a glimpse of a dark room with a patterned tiled floor and a glass cabinet. He took one last glance over his shoulder and with no one around he slipped inside and closed the door.

As his eyes began to adjust to the darkness he could make out many more glass cases, but it was too dark to see what they contained. However, directly to his right was a spiral staircase and at the top of it was a small wall light. Its soft bluish glow illuminated an oval door, and intrigued by the unusual design Archie tiptoed up towards it. He found the door to be made of heavily carved wood with an equally decorative doorknob. As expected, the door was locked and he used the gold key to open it.

Blue light filtered through the crack in the door as he eased it open. He peered into a circular room that was lit by small recessed lights set around the edges of the floor. Windows stretched all the way up to a glass-domed ceiling covered in rain, and beyond it lay the night sky.

To his left was a small brass door recessed in the wall. It reminded him of an oven with its two glass dials. But what really impressed Archie was a huge brass telescope that took up the centre of the room. It was so large, it looked like a giant cannon pointing towards the sky. Even as he stood looking at it, Archie knew this was no ordinary telescope because halfway down it was a glass bubble and at its base were a series of brass wheels and levers. It was irresistible.

He climbed five brass steps that took him up on to the platform on which the telescope stood, then sat down on a viewing stool. He looked through the lens with his blue eye but could see nothing other than thick white mist. He wiped the lens with his sleeve and looked through it again, this time using his green eye. The mist began to clear and he could see grey shifting shapes moving in slow motion.

'What am I seeing?' he mumbled, and a voice whispered, '*He who has vision sees beyond the horizon.*'

Archie pulled away from the telescope and his eyes searched the room. 'Who's there?'

Yet, even as he asked the question, he knew the voice had come from somewhere other than inside the room. This was the I.C.E. headquarters and, as Miss Napier had said, nothing was ever as it seemed and to always expect the unexpected. He returned his green eye to the telescope and the mist and the shadows were replaced by a swirling kaleidoscope of colours. He was trying to make sense of it when a thought began to form in his head.

'Give me vision,' he whispered.

The swirling colours cleared and he found himself looking at a turbulent grey sea that was rising and falling like a giant watery roller coaster. He could see the harbour at Westervoe swamped by the waves and he could see a small boat caught in this maelstrom. He spun the wheels at the base of the telescope, searching for a way to enlarge the vision. He lost sight of the boat and, as the waves lashed the lens, a bow reared up in front of him. He could see Rufus leaning over the side, his arms outstretched, reaching for something.

The vision began to fade into a series of coloured dots before bursting into focus again, and this time Archie saw himself standing high above the stormy sea. His arms were crossed in front of his body and he was holding the torch in one hand and the dagger in the other. Archie spun the wheels at the base of the telescope again until he had a clear magnified image of himself. What he saw made him pull away from the telescope. His eyes had been tightly shut as if he was racked with pain and his whole body had been shaking violently. The image so disturbed him that he couldn't bear to look at it any longer. With a thumping heart he stood up and left the room.

He hurried down the spiral staircase and opened the door that led back out into the corridor, but a tall shadow was moving across the wall where someone was descending the stairs.

Archie quickly shut the door and waited for a moment. When he peered out again, the shadow was gone. With the coast now clear, he slipped out of the room, and with the gold key already in his hand he began to lock the door. He was congratulating himself on not getting caught when the corridor was suddenly filled with the piercing wail of a burglar alarm going off.

Chapter Twenty-six

Archie pulled the gold key out of the lock and stood with his back to the door. People were already running out of the reception room and staring at him.

'What's going on?' someone was saying.

'Is it a break-in?' asked someone else.

The corridor was suddenly crowded with people and Cecille appeared out of their midst, hurrying towards him. 'Archie? Are you all right?'

Professor Himes turned towards the man in the dog-tooth jacket who had been talking to Cecille. 'Malcolm? Turn the alarm off. Stanley? Take Gilbert and Monroe and check the premises. Everyone else, please return to your desks and carry out a thorough inspection for signs of intrusion.' Professor Himes pushed his hair back from his forehead and announced, 'We are on high alert.'

Jeffrey was reminded of his own bank 'incident' the night before. 'Has someone called the police?'

Professor Himes was emphatic. 'Absolutely not. We cannot afford to have the police search the building. For a start, how would we explain Miss Napier's trance state? There are also a few other peculiarities to our organisation that may prove difficult for the police to understand. I.C.E. is quite capable of taking care of its own security.'

The alarm was turned off but the jovial atmosphere of the reception had been replaced by staff scurrying between rooms and running up and down the stairs. However, no one attempted to enter the room with the double doors in front of which Archie still stood.

Cecille looked pale and tired. 'I think it's time to call it a night, Jeffrey. I don't imagine anyone is in party mood any more.'

The woman who minutes before had been laughing with Jeffrey appeared at the doorway of the room that held the stacks of newspapers.

'We're all clear in here, Professor Himes.'

'Good, good,' said the Professor.

The man with the handlebar moustache poked his head around the door of the room that looked like a telephone exchange, and said, 'Clean as a whistle in here, too.' He had a walkie-talkie in his hand. 'Gilbert and Monroe confirm all external doors and windows are intact. They're upping security overnight as a precaution.'

'Good. Good,' said the Professor again. 'Tell everyone to clear up now. Get some rest.' He turned to Jeffrey and Cecille. 'Unfortunately, your first visit to I.C.E. will have to be cut short.' Then he turned to Archie. 'I hope it wasn't too boring for you.'

Archie shook his head and said, 'It's been very interesting, thank you.' It most certainly had not been boring. Particularly what he had just seen through the telescope. He wished he could talk to someone about it. He looked around at the people in the corridor. Someone was missing. Cecille had noticed too.

'I wonder where Rufus got to during all this excitement?' she said.

Jeffrey looked at his watch. 'If he wants a lift back in the Land Rover rather than taking the bike, he's got to make an appearance soon. I don't want to hang around much longer. Could be a slow drive back to Westervoe.'

'I wonder if I could call upon you to give me a lift home,' the Professor asked. 'You see, I took my bicycle today, and in this rain . . .'

'Of course we'll give you a lift,' said Cecille. 'Just as soon as Rufus appears.'

'I'll try and locate him,' said Professor Himes. 'Won't be long.'

They watched him stride along the corridor and take the stairs. 'Wonder why he's so sure Rufus is downstairs,' Cecille muttered.

Jeffrey was more interested in the landscape paintings hanging on the corridor walls. 'Come and look at this, Cecille. A Mactaggart!'

Archie left them admiring the paintings and took the stairs down to the ground floor hall. His hearing had become more sensitive since being struck by the energy Miss Napier had been channelling, which was why he could hear whispering voices coming from the basement.

'Do you think it travelled down with you?' Professor Himes was asking.

'No,' Rufus answered. 'I checked and double-checked. Its strength is growing. Westervoe to Edinburgh is nothing to it now.'

Professor Himes sounded concerned. 'Then the prophecy is coming true. *When shadow meets shadow and water burns as fire, I shall return.*'

Shadow and fire. Archie remembered those were the words Cecille had heard Rufus say during his delirious nightmare.

'It was a strong curse,' Rufus was now saying. 'There must have been some residue left after we exterminated it.'

'You're in grave danger, Rufus. Perhaps some help –'

'No! Not after last time. I'll do it on my own.'

Archie heard footsteps behind him. Cecille and Jeffrey were walking down the stairs. Cecille was yawning and

Jeffrey was looking at his watch. 'Any sign of Rufus yet?' he asked. 'Ah! There you are.'

Rufus had appeared at the top of the basement steps, closely followed by Professor Himes.

'Where have you been?' Cecille asked.

'Organising overnight parking,' Rufus told her. 'Decided to come back with you in the Land Rover.'

'Let's go, then,' said Jeffrey. 'It's going to be a slow drive back in this rain.'

They all headed towards the main door, but Archie held back. He was thinking about the Professor and Rufus's whispered conversation.

What he had heard them say explained why he hadn't been invited by I.C.E. to battle the curse activity around Westervoe. Rufus wanted to do it on his own. Archie felt a huge wave of disappointment and removed the medals that had been hanging around his neck. As he put them away in his jacket pocket, he wondered if they really counted for anything at all.

Chapter Twenty-seven

Professor Himes sat in the front seat of the Land Rover giving Jeffrey directions to the Trinity area of the city. Archie sat in the back, squeezed between Cecille and Rufus, who would occasionally turn and look out through the back window.

The Land Rover slowed down as Professor Himes instructed Jeffrey to pull up outside a large house in a Georgian terrace. He was insistent they all come in for a nightcap before going on their way.

'A very quick one, then,' said Jeffrey, who was growing increasingly anxious about the journey back to Westervoe.

The path leading to the front door had overgrown hedges either side of it. The house itself was in darkness, apart from thin shafts of light visible behind the wooden shutters covering the first floor windows. The Professor unlocked the door and they walked into a warm cavernous hall, lit by wall lights, each in the shape of a clam shell. The faded cream and gold wallpaper was concealed by many paintings of seascapes.

They hung up their coats and climbed a wide staircase to the first floor landing. To their immediate right was a dark varnished door which Professor Himes opened.

Archie's first impression of the wood-panelled room was of a captain's cabin. There was a large globe on a stand beside the window, and a well-polished dining table stood in the centre of the room, supporting neat stacks of books. The room was lit by wall-mounted lights in the shape of candles, and soft leather chairs were placed either side of an open fire.

Professor Himes placed a tin he had been carrying on the table and lifted the lid. 'Help yourselves,' he said. Inside the tin were leftover sardine paste sandwiches and, although everyone smiled and said, 'Thank you,' no one attempted to eat one.

Archie was by now peering out into the night through a crack where the window shutters didn't quite meet. There was little to be seen other than the rainwater running down the glass. But he could just make out a watery figure stepping from a taxi as another figure appeared at the gate. They ran up the path together towards the house, talking earnestly.

Archie looked towards Professor Himes, who was measuring sherry into four glasses. He seemed oblivious to the commotion the two figures made as they entered the hall. In fact everyone seemed oblivious to the new arrivals except Archie. Cecille was admiring a painting of Moss Rock, Rufus was trying to tune an old radio and Jeffrey was impressed with a carving of an African tribesman's head.

'Masai,' Professor Himes informed him.

While they were all preoccupied, the door opened and a woman walked into the room wearing a grey raincoat that had wet patches from the heavy rain on the shoulders. In her hand was a matching hat.

'Wilma!' Professor Himes exclaimed. 'I didn't hear you come in. Everyone, let me introduce my wife.'

The woman smiled politely but was clearly in a hurry. 'Pleased to meet you all, but if you'll excuse me for just a moment...' She turned to the Professor. 'Neville, guess who I met outside...?'

And then a second figure entered the room. Professor Himes looked surprised. 'Miss Napier?'

Her glasses were wet and steaming up. Everything about her was apologetic, so that when she spoke it was in a slightly breathless tone. 'I'm sorry to disturb you at home ... but, Professor, I have important news. I was just leaving to get my bus when I felt the most awful pain in my sinuses. I hurried back to the basement, checked the map, and ... I *must* talk with you, Professor. It's *serious*.'

'Serious?'

She leaned closer and he bent down so she could whisper in his ear.

When she finished, he stood up straight and set the sherry bottle down on the table. 'Good grief! Are you sure?'

Miss Napier removed her glasses and wiped them on a handkerchief. 'Been feeling congested for quite some time but it came to a "head", you might say, this evening.' She sneezed. 'I've noted it in the logbook.' She blew her nose and put her glasses on.

Mrs Himes handed her a glass of sherry. 'This may help ease your nasal pressure.'

Miss Napier looked grateful. 'Thank you.' She took a sip of the sherry and then directed her remarks to Professor Himes.

'As you know, I've been busily charting a strong curse front coming in from Eastern Europe. Usually, a front of this type would offload energy en route, thereby reducing its impact. I would have expected to register some weather influences, or perhaps a bit of civil unrest – nothing too serious, but certainly worth noting. However, this has not happened. In fact this energy is still travelling on a determined course, increasing speed and, more worryingly . . . growing stronger.'

She took another sip of sherry.

'Would you like to sit down?' said Mrs Himes. 'And, please, have a sandwich.'

Miss Napier sat down but declined a sandwich.

Then she continued. 'Unfortunately a new factor has entered this worrying equation. You recall I had trouble with aching lower gums?'

Professor Himes nodded.

Miss Napier frowned, gave a pained look and then continued. 'This new factor stems from a second curse front moving in from the west, and with similar characteristics. It's travelling at the same speed, but yet again there is no offload of energy and, similarly, it's growing stronger by the minute.'

She continued to look intently at Professor Himes while trying to gauge his reaction. Professor Himes was equally intense.

'And what is your opinion of this unusual state of affairs?'

Miss Napier took a deep breath and announced, 'We have a Grade 3, touching 4, and growing rapidly stronger. Another forty-eight hours and we'll have an . . .'

Mrs Himes put her hand to her mouth and gasped.

'SC56!'

Professor Himes remained calm. 'Do we have a point of contact, Miss Napier?'

She looked over his shoulder and, as expected,

Jeffrey, Cecille and Archie were all staring at her, intrigued and waiting for her response. Rufus, however, had his arms folded and was staring at the globe.

Miss Napier leaned closer to Professor Himes and he tilted his head again so she could whisper into his ear.

'Can you repeat that a bit more clearly?' he murmured.

The voice that replied was not Miss Napier's.

'The SC56 point of contact is Westervoe.'

Everyone was suddenly looking at Archie. Miss Napier, in particular, was peering over the top of her glasses while waiting for an explanation as to how he knew this top secret information.

'I just heard Miss Napier tell Professor Himes,' Archie explained. Everyone was now looking at Miss Napier for confirmation.

She nodded her head thoughtfully. 'Those were my exact words.'

Jeffrey mumbled that Archie must surely have extra-ordinarily good hearing, and then turned to Miss Napier.

'What exactly is an SC56? Can you explain what this "energy" is?'

Miss Napier chose her words carefully. 'Energy is a collective term I use for curses. The letters "SC" stand for "Severe Curse", which is usually associated with those on a collision course. In this particular instance we expect the forces to fall between the strongest Grades of 5 and 6. Thus the term SC56.'

Jeffrey was trying to understand the situation. 'You say one energy band is –'

'We refer to it as a "front",' Miss Napier corrected him.

Jeffrey continued. 'So one front is coming from the east and another front is coming in from the west?'

Miss Napier nodded. 'That is correct.'

'Is this related to the curse activity currently around Westervoe?'

She nodded again. 'Yes.'

Jeffrey sighed as though his worse suspicions were being confirmed. 'What can we expect from the impact?'

Cecille put a reassuring hand on his arm. 'It doesn't matter, Jeffrey. It's nothing to do with us.' She looked to Professor Himes, Mrs Himes and Miss Napier for confirmation, and when not one of them agreed she turned her attention back to Professor Himes. 'Thank you very much for your hospitality this evening. I wish you well in dealing with this curse "problem", but I think it's time we made our way back to Westervoe.'

'Could be difficult,' said Rufus, who had been quietly listening to the radio. He turned the volume up and the voice of the newscaster was advising everyone to stay at home due to widespread flooding. With no trains running and the Forth Road Bridge closed to traffic until the following day at the very earliest, there were no direct routes north out of Edinburgh.

'The Land Rover will be fine in floods,' Cecille insisted. 'That machine is built for extreme weather conditions.'

'How is it at tackling landslides?' Rufus asked.

Professor Himes tried to calm the situation. 'I'm sure the roads will be open again first thing tomorrow morning. In the meantime, it looks like you're marooned here for the night.'

Chapter Twenty-eight

Archie decided to sleep fully clothed but for his shoes, which he'd left downstairs. He also decided to keep the light on.

He couldn't stop the many thoughts buzzing around in his head, in particular the conversation he had overheard between Professor Himes and Rufus. What was the prophecy they had been discussing? Then there were the images he had witnessed through the telescope at I.C.E., and of course the SC56 that was on its way towards Westervoe. All this brain activity was keeping him wide awake.

He lay staring around the small room. There was just enough space for a wooden chair by the bed and a chest of drawers under the window. Beyond the shutters he could hear the persistent 'shush shush' of the rain.

He could hear footsteps out in the corridor and doors opening and closing. Occasionally the ceiling light would swing gently, creating strange moving shadows on the walls. When he heard distant voices, he got up and opened his bedroom door.

The corridor was in darkness but concerned voices were coming from Professor Himes's study on the floor below.

'He is our *only* chance. He's the *only* one who can do it . . .' the Professor was saying.

Archie tiptoed along the corridor, listening to Professor Himes's explanation. 'When Archie won the battle against Huigor, he acquired a unique ability. We believe that as a result of the lightning strikes passing through his body, Archie has been left with an extra-sensory force field which detects curse activity. It also appears that this force field around his body is capable of repelling and destroying negative energy.'

Archie heard gasps of disbelief coming from the study as he hurried down the stairs. By the time he stood outside the door, Jeffrey was saying, 'Why do I get a bad feeling about all this?'

Cecille's voice was just as anxious. 'I still don't see what all this has got to do with Archie.'

Archie bent down and looked through the keyhole. He couldn't see very much, other than Rufus standing by the window spinning the large globe with his hand.

Professor Himes was talking again.

'Your invitation to I.C.E. this evening served two

purposes. Firstly, that Jeffrey should receive a well-deserved honour for his part in helping to break the Stringweed curse . . . but the invitation was also an opportunity for us to monitor Archie in a relaxed and stress-free situation. The results were interesting. He was able to intercept and tolerate strong curse energy without serious side effects, thanks in part to wearing rubber-soled shoes. We also discovered he has the ability to see beyond the horizon and he has the gift of curiosity without undue recklessness. In short he is our ideal candidate.'

'Candidate for what?' Cecille and Jeffrey asked at the same time.

'Archie, as you know, is a member of I.C.E.,' the Professor explained. 'It is membership of a small and very select group of people who, by having tackled and broken a curse of between Grade 4 and Grade 6, have developed strengths beyond that of a normal individual. In Archie's case, we have yet to determine what he is fully capable of. However, the tests we set him tonight confirm what we suspected. He is a conduit.'

Jeffrey was trying hard to hide his exasperation. 'A conduit?'

'It's a term we use for an individual who can conduct curse energy that would be lethal to anyone else.'

Cecille sounded horrified. 'You mean they would die?'

Professor Himes nodded. 'I appreciate this is difficult for you.'

Jeffrey was trying hard to remain calm. 'How can
you be sure Archie has this ability and that he won't
be . . .' His voice faltered. 'That he won't be killed?'

Professor Himes tried to reassure him. 'Naturally,
we cannot rehearse the effects of an SC56 on Archie.
But we are confident of his ability.'

Cecille wasn't convinced. 'I will not allow Archie to
exterminate another curse, and that is the end of it.
What you expect of him is impossible.'

'Once you accept the impossible, anything is
possible,' the Professor insisted.

'Fine words,' Cecille retaliated, 'but it's not *your* son
that I.C.E. is prepared to sacrifice.'

Professor Himes nodded in agreement. 'Let me put
the situation into context. If the two fronts of the SC56
collide, then the whole of Westervoe could be wiped off
the map. Archie is the only one capable of averting this
tragedy.'

There was an uncomfortable silence that was eventually broken by Professor Himes. 'I would like to call
upon Miss Napier to explain the mechanics of the situation more fully.'

Miss Napier cleared her throat and began to speak in
a slow, modulated voice. 'Huigor was a particularly
powerful and complex curse. It appears he left behind a

void, a black hole, and this hole is drawing curses towards it like a huge magnet. The majority of these curses are insignificant in themselves, and their impact would normally be minimal, but their sheer numbers have combined to strengthen their collective power. Unfortunately, another factor has to be added to this worrying equation. On rare occasions, broken curses have been known to retain a trace of energy, and when this happens they will search for a means to regain their former influence. We believe they are using the power of the approaching curse fronts to do this. If the fronts collide, the impact will not only increase the size of the black hole, but will reactivate dormant curses and return them to their former strength. That is why it is imperative that they are quashed.'

'And if they are not quashed?' Cecille asked.

'Then Huigor will rise again. The Stringweed curse will be reactivated. All Archie went through will have been for nothing.'

Chapter Twenty-nine

Archie had heard enough. He opened the door and walked into the room. Everyone was sitting down except Professor Himes, who was standing by the fire, and Rufus, who was still spinning the globe.

Cecille raised her head out of her hands. 'Archie, what are you doing out of bed?' She stood up and walked towards him.

'Doesn't look as though he's ever been in it,' Jeffrey remarked, taking in Archie's jeans and jumper.

'I want to go back to Westervoe,' Archie announced. 'Tonight.'

'That's not possible –' Cecille started to say.

But Archie was insistent. 'After I battled Huigor, the Icegull told me I would be called upon again –'

'The Icegull told you that?' said Cecille.

Jeffrey was suddenly up out of his seat and standing next to her. 'Now listen here, Archie. We're your parents. We decide what you can and can't do . . . not

170

some bird.'

'I'm a curse exterminator, Dad. There will be other curses to break.' Archie looked at Professor Himes and then Miss Napier. 'Has the time come for my next challenge? Are you inviting me to tackle the SC56?'

Professor Himes took control of the situation. 'First things first, Archie. What did you overhear us say?'

Archie took a deep breath. 'Two energy fronts are on a collision course. One from the east and one from the west. If the fronts collide, then all dormant curses will become active again, including Huigor.'

Miss Napier nodded. 'That pretty much sums it up.'

Professor Himes put his hand on Archie's shoulder and asked, 'How do you feel about the prospect of destroying curse energy even more dangerous than Huigor?'

Archie tried not to look at his anxious parents. 'I heard you say no one is capable of breaking this curse except me. I don't want Huigor coming back.'

Professor Himes stood up straight and pulled his shoulders back. 'In that case, with your parents' permission, I invite you to exterminate the SC56.'

'Hold on. Are you quite sure about this SC56 thing?' Jeffrey asked.

Miss Napier nodded. 'I have been doing this job for thirty-five years. I'm quite sure.'

'Then shouldn't you put out a warning or . . . something?' Cecille asked.

'What we don't want to do is cause unnecessary panic,' Professor Himes told her. 'We certainly can't announce we have an SC56 approaching. For a start no one would believe us.'

Miss Napier was nodding in agreement. 'What we can do in these situations is ask the meteorological office to announce a severe weather warning.'

Cecille looked incredulous. 'A *weather* warning? What good would that do?'

Miss Napier remained calm. 'It will give people the chance to prepare for flooding . . . anything else is anyone's guess.'

'But you say you've been specialising in this sort of thing for thirty-five years. How can it be down to guesswork?'

'Each SC56 is unique. Take the Bubonic plague of the fourteenth century. A classic example of what should have been a simple case of fleas mutated into a much stronger energy stream. The repercussions, as we know, were catastrophic.'

'Do we have your permission?' Professor Himes asked.

Cecille looked helplessly at Jeffrey.

Archie remained focused. 'What will I have to do, Miss Napier?'

'The challenge you face on this occasion is water-based.'

Jeffrey was quick to pick up on her answer. 'What do you mean, "this occasion"?'

A line of sweat lay across Miss Napier's top lip and her cheeks were rosy. 'The whole spectrum of elements must be battled. Huigor was air-based. Water is already racing towards us. Which leaves fire and earth. All elemental groups must be quashed to destroy the black hole.'

Jeffrey was trying to remain calm. 'And when will all this happen?'

'As I explained earlier, curses are season-based. That way the elements are able to thrive and expand. The current spring equinox is drawing them towards the Westervoe area and at an unusually strong pace. We may see a similar situation with fire around the midsummer solstice and then again towards the autumn equinox when earth is dominant. As yet, we can't be sure. Strong curse activity is unpredictable.'

There was an uncomfortable silence in the room.

Archie felt as though everyone was looking at him without meaning to. But he wasn't afraid of what lay ahead. The artefacts would help him, just like last time.

Jeffrey wasn't so confident. 'And how is Archie to battle this SC56?'

Miss Napier answered his question. 'The equation is always different. Curse extermination is intuitive and therefore it is difficult to predict what action will be required. Having said that, I'm still researching –'

'When will you know?' Cecille demanded. 'You say there's only forty-eight hours until the SC56 reaches Westervoe. Don't you think you might be cutting it rather fine, considering a child's life may be at stake?'

Professor Himes intervened. 'Miss Napier has been working on this problem non-stop for the last ten days. It is remarkable that she is able to stand, let alone continue to channel energy.'

Miss Napier's small and tired body suddenly heaved with an unexpected series of sneezes. She seemed confused as she searched her pockets for her handkerchief.

'So tired,' she mumbled and her shoulders shuddered as she blew her nose. 'Fatigue is not conducive to tracking curses. I must allow myself a few hours' sleep.'

Professor Himes nodded sympathetically. 'Perhaps we should all get some rest. There's nothing more we can do tonight.'

But Archie wasn't tired and he certainly didn't feel like sleeping. How could anyone sleep with an SC56 imminent?

He looked at Cecille, whose arms were wrapped around her body to stop herself shivering.

'It's been a long day,' she told him.

He looked at Jeffrey, who was staring at his feet while pacing the room.

'We'll sort it out. Whatever it is, we'll sort it out.'

Archie looked at Rufus, whose eyes had never left the blur of the spinning globe. He had made no attempt to join in the conversation about the impending SC56. And then Jeffrey suddenly stopped pacing the room.

'Reactivated curses?' he mumbled, and he spun round and stared at Rufus as though a serious and very significant thought had just occurred to him. And from the look on his face it wasn't good news.

Chapter Thirty

Archie was dreaming about the herring gull. It was following him, just above his head, and no matter how hard he tried he couldn't get away from its threatening beak or its persistent screech that went on and on and on . . .

He woke up to the wail of an ambulance siren. He could hear other sounds too. Someone out in the corridor was saying, 'Hush, you'll wake Archie.'

He looked at the time on his watch. It was 2.58 a.m. He got up and walked out into the corridor.

'Dad?'

Jeffrey spun round. He was fully dressed and, oddly, wearing his outdoor jacket. Standing beside him was a very concerned-looking Professor Himes wearing a navy dressing gown and tartan slippers. His hair was sticking out at odd angles and behind him Mrs Himes was hurrying towards the stairs, pulling on a floral bathrobe.

'What's happening?' Archie asked.

Jeffrey put his hands on Archie's shoulders. 'Now there's nothing to worry about. Mum's not feeling too well. Could be something she ate.'

The ambulance siren was growing steadily louder. 'Where is she?' Archie asked.

'Downstairs. I'm taking her to hospital. Just as a precaution, you understand? We'll be back in no time.'

The siren now sounded as if it was on the street outside the house.

'I want to come with you,' Archie told him.

Jeffrey looked over his shoulder towards the stairs as the siren fell silent. 'It's best if you stay here.' He turned back to Archie. 'Please.'

Unrecognisable voices were now talking in the hall and Archie ran towards the stairs.

'I want to see Mum.'

Two medics were leaning over Cecille, who was sitting on a chair, huddled in her coat and rocking back and forth with pain. Mrs Himes was crouched in front of her holding her hand.

'I don't want to go to hospital,' Cecille was telling them. 'I have to take Archie back to Westervoe. I can't be ill. Not now.'

'Mum?'

Cecille looked up and tried smiling. 'I think it was the fish paste sandwiches.' She winced and resumed her rocking.

'Can I come to the hospital with you?' Archie asked.

She shook her head. 'Wait here with Rufus. It won't take long.'

The medics nodded in agreement. 'She'll be back before you know it.' Even so, they put her in a wheelchair and draped a blanket over her knees and shoulders.

Jeffrey drew Rufus aside. 'I don't know how long this is going to take . . .'

Cecille overheard his remark. 'We'll be back by morning,' she insisted. 'Archie won't face the SC56 on his own.' Just saying this made her sigh with pain.

A medic tried calming the situation. 'Let's wait and see what the doctors have to say, shall we?' He turned to Archie and smiled. 'What's this SC56? School exam, is it?'

'An exam of sorts, I suppose,' Archie said as the other medic opened the front door.

The night outside was a black watery blur but for the ambulance lights at the end of the path. Cecille grabbed Archie's hand and squeezed it.

'I'll see you in the morning.'

'Wake me as soon as you get back,' he told her.

'I promise,' she whispered but her voice was barely audible above the heavy rain hitting the doorstep.

'Let's go,' one of the medics remarked.

Jeffrey put a comforting arm around Archie's

shoulders. 'You mustn't worry. Everything will be OK.'

Then he opened a black umbrella the Professor had given him and held it over Cecille's wheelchair as she was pushed down the path.

Archie watched the medics lift Cecille inside the ambulance and Jeffrey gave a small wave before climbing in beside her. Then the door was pushed shut.

A cold rain was falling, but it was the eerie wail of the siren that sent a shiver down Archie's spine. As he listened to the ambulance speed away into the night with its blue light flashing, it crossed his mind that it sounded just like a lone gull crying its heart out.

Chapter Thirty-one

It was almost 5 a.m. when Archie heard a voice close to his ear. It was Rufus telling him to get up. Archie's head was fuzzy with broken sleep but one thought in particular was clear.

'Is Mum back?'

Rufus shook his head and Archie closed his eyes in disappointment.

'They're keeping her in for a couple of days for observation,' Rufus explained. 'It's nothing serious. Looks like food poisoning. Probably the fish paste sandwiches. Jeffrey's still at the hospital with her.'

Archie was confused. A gap in the shutters showed it was still dark outside. 'Then why do I have to get up?'

'I'm taking you back to Westervoe. We all think you'd be better off at home.'

'But I thought the bridge was closed. And what about the landslides?'

Rufus winked. 'No problem when you've got an

aeroplane.'

Archie sat up. 'Monika!'

He didn't feel so tired any more. He pushed the quilt aside and swung his legs over the edge of the bed.

'But I thought you rode the motorbike down!'

Rufus handed him his shoes. 'Had an inkling something like this might happen. Conditions weren't too good last night to land Monika at the old Westervoe aerodrome. That's why I arranged overnight parking at the airport. The weather's improved this morning so we should leave now while it's clear.'

Mrs Himes insisted they eat a breakfast of porridge and very hot tea and Professor Himes said he would give them a lift to the airport. He also suggested dropping in on I.C.E. for an update on the SC56 situation.

They could hear Miss Napier sneezing away in the Map Room. They found her in a corner muttering to herself while replacing codicils on the shelves. She spun round when she heard them approach.

'Is it morning already?'

'It's 6 a.m.,' Professor Himes informed her. 'Have you been here all night?'

Miss Napier nodded and sneezed again. 'So much to do.'

'What's the latest regarding the SC56?' he asked. 'Any overnight developments?'

181

Miss Napier nodded again. 'Another strong surge at 3.33 a.m. I am also monitoring unusual sea activity close to Westervoe. I shall keep you informed.'

Professor Himes thanked her for the update and he and Rufus walked out into the corridor to discuss the situation further.

Archie stayed behind, staring up at shelf upon shelf of codicils tied with coloured ribbon.

'How do you put a curse on someone?' he asked.

Miss Napier gasped so loudly her glasses almost fell off. 'Don't say such a thing! The world is already over-loaded with curses. We cannot cope with many more. Not only that, placing a curse drains you of positive energy. Don't even consider it!'

She reached into her skirt pocket. 'Almost forgot, Archie. Found this on the corridor floor when I returned last night.' In her hand was a small folded piece of paper and written in large letters across it was 'To Archie, From Sid'.

'Must have fallen out of your pocket last night when you were thrown to the floor.'

Miss Napier pressed the paper into his hand. He felt a mild static shock and the inside of the room turned to black and white. Miss Napier released his hand and his sight returned to normal. The sudden impairment had been so brief he wondered if it had happened at all. Certainly it appeared to have no effect on Miss Napier, who had turned back to the shelves of codicils.

'Archie?' Rufus called to him from the doorway. 'We're leaving now. Say goodbye to Miss Napier.'

She smiled wearily at Archie. 'Have a safe journey home. And remember, all of us here at I.C.E. are working hard to protect you.' She went to shake his hand but realised she was still holding the damp codicil, which she transferred into her left hand.

'Good luck,' she said and clasped his hand tightly.

Her fingers still felt damp from the wet codicil she had been holding, but even as that thought crossed Archie's mind the room faded to grey. The only colour he could see was Miss Napier's face, which was bathed in a yellowish glow. But what transfixed Archie was the scenario going on behind her.

He realised he was no longer in the Map Room but somewhere else in time. He could hear voices shouting over the screech and whirr of birds and insects. The air was humid and filled with the smell of moist undergrowth. He felt perspiration break out on his forehead and a dull ache climbed up his spine as one of the voices turned to a chilling scream. Then he caught the scent of an animal. A large black creature crept across his vision so he could no longer see Miss Napier. The creature was so tall he could see nothing of it other than its body, but then it crouched to reveal a figure with a dagger in his hand. The man wore a wide-brimmed hat that obscured his face and his clothes were soaked with sweat. He was panting with exhaustion as the animal prepared to pounce. Archie heard a voice somewhere behind him calling, 'Rufus!' and the creature heard it too. It turned and its blood-red eyes looked directly into Archie's . . .

Miss Napier quickly dropped her hand and Archie was returned to the room.

She stared at his shocked expression. 'You saw it, didn't you?'

Archie nodded.

Miss Napier was apologetic. 'I'm so sorry. I should have realised. Tiredness, you see.' She looked at her damp hand. 'The moisture – it conducted curse energy from the codicil into your hand . . .' Her voice turned urgent. 'Listen to me, Archie. It would be better if you didn't reveal what you saw.'

'Why?'

'It was a very difficult time for Rufus, and now with dormant curses resurfacing and the SC56 approaching . . .' She thought for a moment then made a decision. 'It's not my place to say any more. The I.C.E. code of confidentiality forbids it.'

Archie could hear Rufus's footsteps out in the corridor. There wasn't much time. 'The telescope upstairs?' he asked Miss Napier. 'Does it show the future?'

He realised he had just admitted to being in the tele-scope room, but Miss Napier appeared unconcerned, as though she knew already. She was about to answer the question but Rufus was back in the doorway.

'Archie?' he said. 'We should leave.'

'Go now, Archie,' Miss Napier advised. 'Time is not on our side.' Then she glanced at him out of the corner of her eye and whispered, 'What will be, will be.' Archie knew then the telescope had shown him the future.

Archie followed Rufus back along the corridor, past the open doors leading to rooms that contained shelf upon shelf of codicils. Miss Napier had said he must never handle them and now he knew why. By touching her hand, which was still moist from holding the damp codicil, he had unwittingly tapped into the codicil's energy and the knowledge it contained. Miss Napier had inadvertently given him a clue by mentioning the words 'Rufus' and 'resurfacing curses' in the same sentence. He was sure there was a connection between the creature he had just seen and why Rufus was reluc-tant to talk about his past. It also explained Jeffrey's behaviour the night before. How he had suddenly stopped pacing the floor in Professor Himes's study and stared at Rufus, while saying, 'Reactivated curses?' Because Jeffrey had once secretly read Rufus's diary he must have realised, just as Archie did now, that if the SC56 wasn't destroyed it wouldn't just be Huigor returning to haunt the Stringweed family, but Rufus's curse too.

Chapter Thirty-two

Archie sat in the front seat of Professor Himes's car on the drive to the airport. Rufus sat in the back staring out the rear window. The Professor was doing all the talking.

'Expect strong sea turbulence and unusual marine activity as the SC56 closes in,' he told them. 'There will be other effects, too. At the point of collision the SC56 will contain enough energy to produce a time slip. If this should happen it is important to stay focused. Don't allow what you see to break down your concentration. And Archie? It is particularly important that you remember to wear the flying goggles to protect your eyes.'

Rufus turned from staring out the back window to ask one question, 'Won't all this activity attract attention?'

'Most people will be inside sheltering from the weather,' Professor Himes assured him. 'Those unfortunate enough to be out at sea will assume they are seeing a trick of the clouds or unusual tidal patterns, which is possible when there is no visible horizon to give perspective.'

Rufus went back to staring out the back window.

Professor Himes had one more piece of advice. 'Be careful, both of you. Particularly where the pebbles are concerned. To lose them would be catastrophic.' He looked at Rufus through his rear-view mirror. 'Guard them with your life if necessary.'

Archie put his hand in his pocket to check on his pebble, and found Sid's note. He carefully unfolded the piece of paper and read:

I heard Mrs Merriman tell Mr Taylor that
Ruby's mother had phoned to say she was behaving oddly
and sees weird things and tells lies.
Don't tell anybody else.
P.S. My dad's going to give me £2.50 if my slack tooth
comes out before Saturday.

Archie sat quietly considering the information about Ruby all the way to the airport.

While Professor Himes parked the car, Rufus checked and then rechecked the inside of the plane. When Archie asked, 'What are you looking for?' he merely replied, 'Just being thorough.' But Archie thought he appeared nervous.

They said their goodbyes to Professor Himes and Archie handed the Professor his I.C.E. medals on the gold chain. 'Would you give these to my mother?'

Professor Himes looked surprised but quickly composed himself. 'I'll go to the hospital first thing this morning and personally hand them to her.'

The Professor waited at the side of the airfield to wave them off and by the time they were airborne he was a tiny watery figure climbing back into his car.

Archie glanced at Rufus. He was eager to ask about the black creature he'd seen in the vision, but decided to heed Miss Napier's advice and not ask questions – for the time being. But there was still the matter of the Stringweed curse to deal with.

'If a small part of Huigor is still alive and waiting to be reactivated, where do you think he is?' Archie asked.

Rufus considered the question. 'We know Huigor is earthbound and weak, which explains why Miss Napier is having trouble locating him. But once he starts to feed off the approaching SC56 he'll grow in strength and she'll be able to detect his exact whereabouts.'

Archie thought back to the shadow in the school cupboard.

'Could Huigor be in Westervoe?'

'That's my feeling. By being close to the sea he'll be in a better position to feed off water-based curses.'

'Is that why you told me to stay away from the harbour?'

Rufus nodded. 'I sensed curse activity in the area but I didn't want to worry you until I knew for sure. I was also concerned about curse contamination of the water.'

Archie wanted to tell Rufus what he'd seen through the telescope at I.C.E. but that would mean admitting he had used the gold key to get inside the room.

Rufus noticed Archie's concerned expression.

'As a curse exterminator you will experience many strange things,' he told Archie. 'If this should happen, don't panic. Keep a clear head and give yourself time to make a sound judgment. Promise me you will do that.'

'I promise,' Archie told him. And then no more was said by either of them.

Before long they were flying over the Forth Road Bridge. It was empty of traffic, although the approach roads to the bridge were lined with vehicles halted by flood water and the debris of landslides.

On they flew, over flooded roads and fields. Where the night sky had once been, shafts of light were breaking through the low cloud, giving the impression of golden daggers striking Moss Rock.

'I have an idea,' Archie told Rufus. 'When we get home, I'm going to get the flute out of my box of artefacts and call the Icegulls. They'll help us.'

Rufus shook his head. 'We can't rely on the Icegulls

this time. They're still regenerating. It's a renewal process that starts in January and takes at least three months to complete.'

'Are they regenerating on Moss Rock?'

'No one knows for sure where they regenerate, although they always do so in the northern hemisphere. The process is complete when green flickering light appears in the night sky.'

'The Northern Lights?'

'It's similar, but Icegull regeneration is a distinctive fluorescent green.'

Archie looked down at the imposing cliffs of Moss Rock. 'So we're on our own this time.'

'I'm afraid it looks that way.'

Rufus dropped altitude and flew Monika around to the other side of Moss Rock where the cliffs faced the open ocean. 'Might as well take a look at the sea since we're here. Just in case there are any signs of unusual marine activity.'

They saw nothing out of the ordinary and Rufus swung the plane round. They were heading back towards Moss Rock when Monika gave a violent shudder. Rufus looked at the control panel.

'We're losing power. I don't understand.'

He gave the engine another thrust but the plane continued to drop, coming to a halt approximately fifteen metres above the sea. They were left suspended in mid-air and beneath them a band of rippling water was rapidly turning into a heaving mass of black and grey bubbles. Tall water spouts shot upwards out of this water to engulf the aircraft and when the windows cleared they found themselves looking out on to six long black necks swaying close to the plane.

'What's happening?' Archie asked.

'Serpents!' Rufus said. 'Find my rucksack. Quickly!'

Archie clambered into the back of the cockpit while Rufus fought to keep control of the shuddering plane.

'Get the knife from the front pocket,' Rufus was now telling him. 'Then hand me the rope and harness from the back seat.'

Archie did what he was told, but it was difficult. The curse activity was making his fingers and toes tingle. Rufus attached one end of the rope to the harness and the other to a metal hoop welded to the cockpit ceiling.

'Now sit here and hold the controls,' Rufus said as he pulled on the harness.

'What are you going to do?' Archie asked.

'I'm going outside.'

'No!'

'Listen to me, Archie. We've got three minutes. That's how long it takes the serpents to perform their challenge dance. I've got to get out there before they finish. I've no choice.'

He opened the cockpit door. 'Whatever you do,

don't let go of the controls, and don't look into the serpents' eyes. They'll make you forget who you are.'

Rufus placed the knife between his teeth and jumped out. He gripped hold of the rope before it reached its full length and snapped him back up again. He was swung through the air in a wide arc close to the serpents, but they were more interested in tempting Archie to look into their eyes as they swayed back and forth in front of the aeroplane windows.

Archie was focused on the control panel, holding the plane steady each time it was rocked violently by the lunging serpents. If Rufus was trying to kill them he'd better hurry because the serpents had gathered outside the open cockpit door. They were performing a complicated swaying movement that involved intertwining their necks to create a powerful six-headed creature. They were now so close he could have reached out through the open door and touched them.

Archie tightened his grip on the controls and wished Rufus would hurry up and do something. He was wondering if the three minutes were up when the aeroplane shuddered and a serpent stuck its head in through the open cockpit door. Archie closed his eyes. He could feel the gaping mouth beside him and the stench of its breath on his face. Then his worst fear was realised when the serpent gripped his arm in its mouth.

Archie's body jolted as the serpent bit into his force

field. He felt as if he had been hit by a torpedo and the air was knocked from his lungs. His eyes flicked open and he found himself inside a glowing shower of white sparks that filled the cockpit and welded his hands to the controls.

The plane shuddered from the force of the writhing serpent. Beyond the dazzling white light he could see the silhouettes of five serpents' heads, their mouths open, their bodies rigid from the anti-curse force Archie was generating. Amid another shower of sparks the serpent's head was jolted free of his arm and Archie found himself looking into a watery dead eye. There was no sound as the creature slid out of the cockpit, pulled down into the sea by the other dead serpents.

The static charge inside the cockpit fizzled and died and Archie heard the welcome sound of the engine firing up. They were suddenly flying again, which was good news, but where was Rufus? Had the sea serpents got him or was he still hanging from the rope? Archie tilted the plane's nose up so they were climbing, but he had also unintentionally sent it heading towards Moss Rock.

He didn't know anything about flying other than what he'd learned from watching Rufus. He certainly didn't know how to land Monika. He looked at the control panel. What was it Rufus had said? 'Don't panic. Keep a clear head. Make a sound judgment.'

That was all very well, but Moss Rock was drawing closer.

'What do I do? What do I do?' he cried out.

'Shove over,' came the reply. Rufus hauled himself up into the plane and grabbed the controls. His clothes were wet and he was still attached to the rope as he manoeuvred the aircraft through a sharp turn until they were almost flying on their side along the length of the cliffs. When they were clear of the rock and heading out to open sea, he tilted Monika again and the open door swung shut. When it was secure, he took one look at Archie, who was clutching the edge of his seat as though he had just been round a roller coaster ten times. His hair was standing on end and he was wide-eyed.

'You can relax now,' Rufus told him.

Archie wasn't ready to relax. 'You left me to be eaten by serpents!'

'Sorry, old chap, but there's no way I would have survived curse energy of that strength.'

Archie was confused. 'I thought you were going to kill the serpents. What was the knife for?'

'To cut myself free if the plane crashed,' Rufus replied.

'Crashed . . .?' Archie whispered.

Rufus tried to reassure him. 'You did everything right, Archie. You kept your head. Destroyed the serpents and saved my life. Thought I'd come a cropper a couple of times though when you started flying the plane.' He smiled, but Archie was still too shocked to notice.

'I thought serpents didn't exist,' Archie managed to say. 'I thought they were just folklore.'

'Oh, they exist all right. Where there's strong water-based curse activity you'll find serpents. Just like Jellats. You see, serpents store negative curse energy and then use it as a means of attack. I've seen them sink boats before but as far as I know there's no record of them attacking an aeroplane. In which case, was it mere chance we came across them or were they waiting to ambush us in the hope of getting the pebbles? Whichever, we've just had a taste of the growing power of the SC56.'

Rufus rubbed his face with a hand as if to wipe away the memory of what had just occurred. Then he turned his attention to the great expanse of sea beneath them and, unable to hide his unease, said, 'I wonder what else is down there waiting for us.'

Chapter Thirty-three

It was raining heavily by the time they came in to land. Large pools of water lay at the side of the runway and the disused hangar looked even more broken and forgotten. As the plane taxied towards the hangar, Archie watched the rain running down the windscreen.

If the serpents were anything to go by, then he was starting to appreciate Professor Himes's remark that the SC56 was even more powerful than Huigor.

They parked Monika and Rufus put on Grandpa Stringweed's old waxed coat and helmet and climbed on to the motorbike. Archie pulled on the spare helmet and squeezed into the sidecar.

They set off along a bumpy track that would eventually take them to the top of Brinkles Brae, and from there it was only a short ride down the hill to Windy Edge. The herring gull flew alongside all the way to the house, then soared up and settled on the chimney pot above Archie's skylight window. From there it watched them park the bike.

When Archie came to open the gate, he noticed the brass name plate was so tarnished it had turned grey. The moss that had been patchy the day before now covered the path all the way up to the front doorstep. He also noticed the house lights were switched on. When they walked into the hall, he could hear the sound of television coming from the living room and the kitchen.

'I left the lights and the TVs on as a precaution. Bright electrical light and sound deter some curse energies,' Rufus explained. 'Thought it best to be on the safe side while we were away.'

There was also a strong smell of damp in the house that hadn't been there the day before, and Archie could hear the trickle of running water, too.

Rufus set off along the hall and came to an abrupt halt just inside the kitchen door. 'What . . .!'

Archie caught up with him and they both stood looking at the cold water tap dripping into an overflowing sink, but it was the remains of a dead rat hanging over the edge of the sink that shocked them. Its eyes had been gouged out, its skull was smashed and very little flesh remained on its skeleton but for the long tapered tail.

Archie followed Rufus towards the sink. 'Mum was

right. A rat was blocking the drain.'

'Then why isn't the water draining away now?' Rufus observed. An unexpected splash in the water stopped them in their tracks and a green and brown tentacle swept the surface before disappearing down into the drain.

'A Jellat?' Archie said. 'They're trying to get into the house.'

Rufus turned off the dripping tap. 'They're just trying to warn us off by showing what their teeth are capable of.' He took a metal skewer out of a drawer and poked it down through the plughole. Bubbles shot up through the water and seconds later the water began to drain away.

'As we can see from the Jellat's calling card, electrical fields don't repel all curse energies,' Rufus said.

Archie and Rufus both grimaced as they looked at the chewed rat.

'OK. Let's get this place cleaned up,' Rufus decided. 'You start on the floor while I dispose of the rat.'

Archie went back out into the hall and was pulling the mop out of the cupboard when the phone rang. He was expecting to hear his mother's voice but instead a girl was saying, 'What time are you coming to tea?'

Archie had forgotten all about Ruby's invite to Ormleigh House that afternoon. With an SC56 on its way, he didn't think going for tea was appropriate.

'I can't come,' he told her. 'I've got things to do.'

Rufus popped his head around the kitchen door. 'Go out if you want. There's nothing more we can do today. From now on it's a waiting game.'

Archie interrupted Ruby's disappointed remarks. 'I can come after all,' he told her. 'What time's good for you?'

'We can pick you up at 3.45 and drop you back home around seven. Olivia wants to know if you have any food allergies.'

Archie said he didn't think so but tapioca made him feel sick and he didn't like thin gravy. Ruby assured him they wouldn't be eating either and soon after they hung up.

He had been disappointed not to hear his mother's voice, but then again he would have another opportunity to ask Ruby about the cursed lion that was supposed to have eaten her father but of which Miss Napier knew nothing. He set about mopping up the wet kitchen floor and as the water swirled around the mop head he thought about Sid's note. If Ruby was imagining things and telling lies that might explain her story about the cursed lion, but it didn't explain how she knew about Jellats, and that was another question he intended to find the answer to that afternoon.

Chapter Thirty-four

Ormleigh House was an old mansion set back off the road. All you could see of it through the trees were tall chimney stacks and a single turret. It was said to be haunted.

Archie felt apprehensive as Olivia's car pulled through the front gates into the long drive. Over-hanging branches clattered against the roof and the car swerved to avoid flooded potholes.

At the top of the drive they came upon a clearing and there before them was the grand façade of the house, but it was a side entrance the car pulled up at, and it didn't look grand at all. Brown paint was peeling from the door and two rubbish bins stood against the outside wall.

Ruby opened the car door and she and Olivia each grabbed a bag of shopping before dashing through the rain towards the house. Archie followed, accompanied by a grey cat that had been sheltering under a wheelbarrow. Together they ran through the open door and into a wood-panelled corridor with a flagstone floor. Archie shut the door and wiped his feet on the mat, while the cat tiptoed down the corridor, shaking the rain from its paws and mewing loudly as it followed Olivia and Ruby into the kitchen.

It was a gloomy room, brightened only by the glow of hot coals in the grate and a vase of daffodils on the window sill. A shelf ran all the way around the walls displaying decorated plates and there was a rocking chair next to the fire. Olivia switched on an overhead light, but it didn't do much to dispel the dreariness.

The house had a strange smell to it, too. It reminded Archie of Norrie Bews's abandoned boatshed, smelly cleaning cloths and cold vegetable soup. Maybe it was the smell of ghosts?

Ruby set her carrier bag down on the table and turned to Archie. 'OK. Let's go,' and they were on the move again.

'We'll eat around 5.30,' Olivia called to them as Ruby led the way through a door at the opposite end of the kitchen.

This time Archie found himself in a grand entrance hall, large enough to accommodate a red velvet sofa and a long polished table that held ornaments and plants. Imposing portraits stared down at him from the walls, men and women dressed in dark clothes and with waxy faces, long dead but who, according to village gossip, still stalked the house at night.

Ruby was already running up the winding staircase. She stopped and looked back at him. 'What's wrong? Scared of ghosts?'

'No!'

'Good,' she told him, 'because there's lots of them in this house.' She continued running up the stairs. '*And* I've seen a black phantom at the crossroads.'

Archie caught up with her outside a door with a sign pinned to it saying 'Ruby's Room. Knock Before Entering'.

She knocked on the door and walked in. Archie went to follow but Ruby barred his way with her arm.

'Can't you read? Knock before entering!'

Archie gave the door a knock and followed Ruby inside.

She switched on the light and the first thing he noticed in the spacious room was an oil painting of Ork Hill hanging over the fireplace. There was an electric guitar propped against a chair, a large dresser with eight drawers, and beneath the window, which looked on to the drive, was a window seat. Archie's attention was quickly drawn towards a glass tank on the table next to Ruby's bed. He remembered her saying she kept terrapins.

'Close the door,' Ruby told him.

Archie was getting fed up of being bossed around, but he shut the door. When he turned round, he found her staring at him.

'Can you keep a secret?' she asked.

'I don't know. What kind of secret?'

'There's something I want to show you, but only if you can keep a secret.'

'I can keep a secret,' said Archie, who as a member of I.C.E. was managing to keep the biggest secret of his life.

Ruby walked over to the terrapin tank and removed the lid. 'Come and look at this.'

Archie watched her pick up a long knitting needle and use it to poke behind the stones piled up at the back of the tank. Something moved. At first Archie thought it was a clump of seaweed but then a pair of glassy black eyes peered out of a floating mass of tentacles.

He had to bite his tongue to stop himself saying, 'A Jellat!' Instead he simply asked, 'What's that?'

'*That* is a Jellat and not a mermaid,' she informed him. 'I caught it in my fishing net before Mr Taylor made his silly rule about not going out to the caves.'

'Has anyone else seen it?'

'Just my mother. She thinks it's seaweed.' She pulled flakes of fish food out of her trouser pocket and sprinkled them on to the water. 'The undersides of their tentacles glow in the dark and they don't live long out of water. You have to be quick when you catch them.'

'How do you know?'

'Because the first one I caught died. I accidentally dropped it on the rocks and it turned into this sludgy brown foam. It was disgusting.'

Archie crouched down to take a closer look at the strange creature. 'What happened to your terrapins?' he asked as he noticed two empty terrapin shells.

'The Jellat ate them. Didn't like the shells though.'

'What else does it eat . . . besides terrapins?'

'Anything. Fish food flakes, sausages, broccoli, bacon. It even ate a pencil. Its teeth are incredibly sharp. I'll show you.'

She picked up a length of string and dangled it just above the water. A split second later a tentacle pulled it into the water and the Jellat's small razor-sharp teeth sliced through it.

'We can go to the caves tomorrow since there's no school,' Ruby was now saying. 'I'll show you exactly where I caught it. If you catch one you can keep it in my tank.'

'Stay away from the caves,' Archie told her. 'It's dangerous there.'

'Don't tell me you're scared.' Ruby didn't wait for a reply. She was already making other plans. 'Oh well, I'll just have to ask George. He doesn't strike me as the unadventurous type.'

Archie was too interested in the Jellat to be bothered by her comment.

'What are you going to do with it?' he asked.

Ruby shrugged. 'Don't know.' They both stood looking at it and then Ruby said, 'It can sing.'

She picked up her recorder from the window seat and began to play 'Greensleeves'. Archie watched the Jellat float close to the surface and open its mouth. Ruby stopped playing the recorder and the creature began to make a sound Archie immediately recognised as the wailing he had heard down at the beach and out at the Point. The individual notes sounded as though they were coming at him from the four corners of the room. One minute they were behind his ear, then above his head, and then close to his ankles, and he felt as if they were pulling him into the tank. He couldn't resist, even if he wanted to, and as his eyes began to close he had to fight the sensation of his mind starting to empty.

But a sudden splash of water hitting his face made him open his eyes. Ruby was standing over the tank, her recorder dripping wet where she had hit the surface of the water with it. The Jellat had darted back behind the pile of stones and was no longer singing.

Ruby gave an impatient sigh and threw the recorder on to the bed. 'I don't like its singing. Gives me a headache.'

'But how do you know that's a Jellat?' Archie asked her. 'Have you ever seen one before?'

'No. But I recognise it from a picture.'

Archie was intrigued. 'Can I see it?'

'Why do you want to see a picture when you can look at the real thing?'

'How do I know it's the real thing?'

'Can't you take my word for it?'

Archie thought back to the note Sid had given him. 'I'm not sure.'

'What do you mean, you're not sure?'

'You said your father was killed by a lion in the jungle . . .'

'Yes.'

'But lions don't live in the jungle.'

Ruby's blue eyes sparkled with indignation. 'I know that. Do you think I'm stupid? The lion was a freak of nature. It wasn't supposed to be there.'

'But it was black!'

'Cursed lions are black!'

'There are no recorded instances of cursed lions, even black ones, killing anybody in a jungle.'

'How do you know?'

'Because I checked with –' Archie realised he had said too much. 'What I mean is I did some research.'

Ruby put her hands on her hips and with her voice rising again said, 'Do you think I would lie about something like that?'

'Then prove it. Show me the picture of a Jellat.'

'No!'

'Why not?'

'It's confidential.'

Archie decided he'd had enough of Ruby's bizarre behaviour.

'Then why tell me about it in the first place! You don't have a picture of a Jellat at all, do you? It's just another lie.'

Ruby was now shouting. 'I do not tell lies, Archie Stringweed!'

'Then prove it!'

'NO!'

The argument was interrupted by a high-pitched wail that filled the room.

They both stopped shouting and looked towards the tank. The Jellat was floating near the surface and was staring at them with its beady little eyes.

'I'm going home,' Archie told her. 'I can't believe a thing you say.'

Ruby looked as if she was about to burst with anger as he walked out the room. He was approaching the stairs when he heard her voice behind him. 'I HOPE THE PHANTOM AT THE CROSSROADS GETS YOU!' she shouted before the door slammed shut.

Archie ran down the stairs and hurried into the

kitchen. To his relief Olivia wasn't there, but the grey cat was up on the table, chewing on a piece of raw meat it had pulled out of a carrier bag. The sound of bone crunching against bone made him think of the mangled rat and Jellats' teeth. When he opened the back door on to the rainy night, he heard an animal howling. The trees were creaking too and the shape of the car parked outside was like a huge predator waiting to pounce.

Archie followed the muddy path all the way round to the front of the house, which was in darkness apart from the light shining in Ruby's first floor bedroom window. He carried on running and had almost reached the end of the drive when he heard the sound of a motorbike approaching. He found the energy to run that bit faster but the motorbike and sidecar sped by just as he reached the gates.

Archie stood breathless watching the yellow beam of the headlamp fade into the distance. Soon after he heard the engine braking and the bike turned down a side road, which confirmed his suspicions. Rufus was on his way to the Point.

He thought about following him, but it was almost dark and in any case it was too far to walk in the heavy rain. He glanced back down the drive towards Ormleigh House. Ruby was nowhere to be seen but Olivia might come looking for him in the car, so he took a deep breath and began to run in the direction of home.

He hadn't gone far when his legs began to feel heavy with the effort of negotiating the deep pools of water at the side of the road. Eventually, he had to content himself with a half-jogging, half-walking rhythm while trying to ignore the sharp ache that had appeared in his side. He told himself that every step forward was taking him further away from Ormleigh House, but then again, each step was taking him closer to the crossroads, which, according to Ruby, was the site of a strange black phantom. Archie decided to take a brief rest because once he started running again nothing was going to make him stop until he was well beyond the crossroads.

But his rest was short-lived. A car was fast approaching from behind and he crouched down behind a clump of long grass at the side of the road. The vehicle raced around the bend, spraying him with water, and once it had driven by he raised his head to catch a glimpse of Olivia's white car. Its headlights lit up the crossroads just long enough to show him there was no phantom creature waiting.

Archie stood up, wiped the water from his face and began to run with his head down against the rain. He kept telling himself that phantoms were nothing compared to being sucked up inside a tornado and struck by lightning. He told himself the howling he could now hear was nothing compared to Huigor's roar.

The darkness, together with the huge raindrops sticking to his eyelashes, made it difficult to see where he was going. He raised a hand and wiped the water from his face and as he looked up he was met with the sight of a creature just up ahead in the middle of the road. It was the size of a large dog and its two red eyes were staring out of a thick black mane. It gave a low growl and opened its mouth to reveal savage yellow fangs. Was this creature Ruby's phantom? The way it was baring its teeth and growling was not in the least ghostly, but looked very real indeed.

Archie was on the point of turning and running back towards Ormleigh House when up ahead, behind the menacing red eyes, he saw something white moving towards him on the road. Olivia's car, he thought, and felt instant relief at being rescued, but in the time it took him to realise the white shape had no headlights, it had already covered the entire width of the road. It took him even less time to realise it was not a vehicle at all, but something much more mysterious.

Chapter Thirty-five

Archie could no longer hear the rain falling around him. Nor could he see where he was going because he was enveloped in a thick white mist. He shuffled towards the grass verge, which should have only taken a few steps, but he soon realised, when he couldn't find it, that he had lost all sense of direction. A wrong turn could take him away from home or straight into the jaws of the creature, but Archie decided it was best to keep on moving rather than do nothing at all. He continued to edge his way slowly along the road, listening and watching for the beast, while also trying to work out his own whereabouts.

The thick mist began to swirl and he could hear muffled sounds above his head. The air moved against the back of his neck and he heard the panting breath of an animal.

He spun round. There was no phantom to be seen, but the mist had changed. It was no longer dense and white but clear and consisted of millions of suspended raindrops, as if the rain had stopped falling mid-air.

He raised his hand to move the raindrops aside and a large ball of liquid formed in his palm. Inside it he could see moving water. He added another handful of drops to this ball and realised that he could see part of a wave. It occurred to him that if he could fuse all the raindrops together then he would see the full picture. But that would be impossible. For a start, he couldn't reach them all.

But as he stood staring at the raindrops he was reminded of the coloured dots he had seen through the telescope at I.C.E. Perhaps there was a way of seeing the bigger picture after all. He covered his blue eye with his hand, and even before he had finished saying, 'Give me vision,' the individual drops fused together to form a clear and towering picture.

Archie found himself surrounded by grey threatening sea and from behind a large wave the torch and dagger rose up. They were crossed like swords, and as they sped towards him they grew in size until the dagger was as long as a lamp post and the torch was as thick as a tree. Still they kept coming at an alarming speed and just as he thought they would crash into him, Archie dropped his hand from his eye.

He found himself back amongst the suspended raindrops. They had lost their colour and were beginning to fall again as rain. The mist, too, had lifted and he could once again see where he was. There was no need to worry about the black creature, because the crossroads were a long way behind him and he found, to his relief, that he had been walking in the direction of Westervoe. Directly ahead was the familiar school building and it seemed to him that its brightly lit windows were inviting him inside.

Archie looked at his watch. It was 4.27 p.m. Rufus would not be expecting him home until seven o'clock. He gripped the gold key tightly in his hand and decided he had the perfect opportunity to find out what was lurking inside the art store cupboard.

Entering the school was straightforward. There was no one around except the cleaners and they were in the cloakroom. Archie could hear them talking and laughing loudly over the clatter of buckets and a radio playing. There was a strong scent of disinfectant that couldn't hide the smell of mould and dampness.

Archie slipped unnoticed into the corridor but he was leaving telltale footprints on the newly washed floor. He removed his trainers and carrying them in his hand he hurried towards his classroom.

As soon as he opened the door, Archie felt a blast of hot air. The fan heater the janitor had placed in the room was circulating the unbearably strong stench coming from the fungus on the ceiling. Long strands of mucus were dripping from it on to the floor, and Archie had the uncomfortable feeling that he was being watched as he set his shoes down on Mr Taylor's desk. With a mixture of fear and expectation, he approached the art cupboard and carefully opened it using the gold key.

Before him were shelves of coloured paper, poster paint, scissors and tubs of glue – but no shadow. He was carefully moving aside a box of scissors when a loud thud made him spin round. On the floor behind him a large piece of the fungus had fallen away and was now lying in a pool of water. Archie looked up at what remained of the fungus on the ceiling and found to his surprise that it was hollow, like a cocoon. A shiver rippled down his back, making the hairs on his neck bristle, and then, out of the corner of his green eye, he glimpsed a movement across the room. He turned and his eyes immediately rested on the fan. A black shadow was rising up in front of the rotating blades and, as he continued to watch, it formed into the unmistakable shape of a small tornado.

Chapter Thirty-six

'Archie?' someone was saying at the open classroom door. 'What are you doing?'

Archie kept his eyes on the funnel-shaped shadow while he said, 'Forgot something. Came back to get it.'

'Stinks in here,' the voice was now saying and Sid walked into the room. He was standing directly behind the fan, which meant he was unable to see the small tornado spinning in front of it.

Another voice asked, 'What are you doing here, Archie?' and Sid's mother walked in dragging a vacuum cleaner. She didn't wait for an answer before exclaiming, 'How am I supposed to work in this smell!' She promptly turned off the fan and without the rotating air the small tornado fell to the floor and drifted out through the classroom door.

Archie moved to follow it but Sid's mother was now saying, 'That's odd. The art cupboard is usually kept locked.' She shut the door and locked it. 'It's not like

Mr Taylor to be so slapdash.' She removed the key and examined it. 'If I didn't know any better I'd say it was made of gold.'

Archie stretched out his hand. 'I'll give the key to Mr Taylor tomorrow.'

'Sorry, Archie. Can't allow a key to leave the school. I'll just put it here on his desk.' She placed it in the paperclip dish next to Archie's wet trainers. 'What on earth are wet shoes doing on the table?' and she looked down at Archie's feet.

'I forgot my wellies,' he told her. 'Didn't want to put muddy marks on the classroom carpet.'

Sid's mum picked up the soggy shoes and handed them to Archie. 'Bad luck to put shoes on a table. And you'll have more chance of finding your wellies in the cloakroom.' She eyed him suspiciously. 'How's your mum?'

'Fine.'

'I'm only asking because I heard your dad wasn't at the bank today, so I thought she might be ill.'

Archie couldn't stop his eyes flicking across to the paperclip dish. It was so close he could have picked up the key if Sid's mum hadn't been watching him so carefully. She was still talking too.

'I suppose your mum's got your Uncle Rufus to look after her if she's a bit under the weather. It'll give him something to do.'

Archie stopped looking at the key and glared at her. 'Rufus has plenty to do. He is always very busy.'

'A bit like myself!' she replied. 'Except I just can't find time to go wandering around the Point late at night.'

Archie was just about to tell her to mind her own business when he heard a loud thud, like someone falling out of bed. What was left of the fungus had dropped from the ceiling, narrowly missing the fish tank.

Sid's mum gave a horrified scream as purple-coloured fumes poured from the fungus, and when Sid took a step closer for a better look she grabbed his arm.

'It's toxic. Let's get out of here before we're poisoned!' She ushered them towards the door and Archie looked back at the small glass paperclip dish on Mr Taylor's desk. He would have to find a way back into the room, but already the other cleaners were hurrying along the corridor towards them.

'What's going on?' one of them asked.

Sid's mother pointed to the classroom. 'It's a health hazard in there.'

Archie was growing more and more agitated. His eyes were searching the corridor for the shadow while frantically trying to find a reason to get back into the room to reclaim his key. Then small sweaty fingers pressed something into his hand.

'It is gold, isn't it?' Sid whispered.

Archie nodded.

Together they ran off down the corridor, and didn't stop until they reached the the main entrance.

'Where did you get a gold key from?' Sid asked.

'I can't tell you, Sid.'

'I can keep a secret, you know.' His voice was small with hope. 'You're the only person I told about Ruby. Did you find my note?'

Archie nodded.

'I put it in your coat pocket,' Sid told him. 'I didn't want George getting his hands on it. He doesn't like Ruby but that's just because she likes you . . .'

While Sid continued to chat on, Archie was wishing he could confide in him. Tell him he was going to have to exterminate another curse and a big one too, as big as they get, an SC56 – but he was sworn to the I.C.E. code of confidentiality, which could not be broken, even for Sid.

'How come your gold key fitted the art cupboard lock?' Sid was now asking.

'It was just luck,' Archie told him.

'Were you going to steal something? If you need money I'll lend you some once my tooth falls out.' He wiggled it. 'Should be some time soon.'

Archie shook his head. 'No. I don't need money.'

Sid shrugged and walked away. 'I've got to empty the

waste-paper baskets.'

Archie zipped up his jacket and opened the door. A cold breeze appeared from the corridor and circled his head and a black shadow drifted outside with a soft moan.

He thought back to Huigor's prophecy inside the tornado as the Stringweed curse was being exterminated. *Where the night and shadows meet, there shall I lie.*

As Archie stood on the school steps staring out into the shadows, he wondered in which dark corner of Westervoe Huigor was lying in wait for him.

Chapter Thirty-seven

By the time Archie opened the gate to Windy Edge he was shivering and he was hungry. Rufus had left all the house lights on again, which should have made the house look welcoming. The cloud of Icegull breath hovering above the roof and the gull perched on the chimney pot should have been reassuring, too, but Archie felt unsettled. Apart from the patter of rain, there was an eerie silence as he walked up the slippery garden path. He had reached the doorstep and the key was already in his hand when the tree gave an unexpected creak and the hedge rustled. Then he heard the click of the garden gate. He looked over his shoulder to see it swing open in a sudden breeze, and when next door's dog began to bark and the gull gave a loud hurried cry, Archie quickly let himself into the house and slammed the door shut. His heart was still pounding as he hung up his coat and kicked off his wet shoes.

There was still an underlying smell of dampness, even though the heating was on and he and Rufus had dried out the kitchen the best they could. It was quiet, too, and to fill the silence he switched on the kitchen television. He was pouring himself a bowl of cereal when the phone rang.

He answered it and a familiar voice asked, 'Archie! How are you?'

Hunger and disappointment temporarily disappeared. 'Dad! I'm fine. How's Mum?'

'She felt a lot better after Professor Himes turned up with your I.C.E. medals.'

Archie tried to sound cheerful but his act faltered when he asked, 'When are you coming home?'

Jeffrey said that if the doctors allowed it, they would be home the following day. In good time before the SC56 struck. 'This is a tricky situation,' Jeffrey explained. 'Best not to tell Grandma or Grandpa that Mum's in hospital, or even that we're in Edinburgh. It could get too complicated. For a start, how do we explain I.C.E.?' Archie was about to say he didn't know but Jeffrey kept on talking. 'I phoned the bank. Said I had to take a couple of days off. If anyone phones just say I'm in bed with flu . . .'

Jeffrey was talking as if he was in a hurry and Archie knew he'd have to be quick if he was to ask the question that was on his mind.

222

'Dad? When are we going on our camping trip up Ork Hill? You promised we would after I broke the Stringweed curse.'

Jeffrey hesitated. 'Might have to put it off for a while. Got a lot on my plate at the moment.'

'But, Dad –'

'Listen, Archie. I'm using the hospital payphone and there's a queue. We'll talk about the trip when I get home. In the meantime, I don't want you to worry about a thing. We'll deal with the SC56 together. Just hang on in there until tomorrow.'

'OK.'

'Lots of love from us both. Mum says be sure to have an early night.'

Archie said he would, and no sooner had he replaced the handset than he heard the motorbike pull up outside and footsteps approach the door. Rufus walked in carrying a package under his arm and there was the irresistible smell of chips. He didn't look surprised to see Archie and he didn't ask how he had unlocked the front door. He just smiled and said, 'I thought you might be hungry. Still no fresh fish, I'm afraid. The shoals won't return until the Jellats are gone, so it's chicken.'

Archie followed Rufus into the kitchen and watched him set the parcel of food on the table.

'Have you been out at the Point?' Archie asked.

Rufus nodded as he washed his hands at the kitchen sink. 'The Jellats are congregating around the caves. Thousands of them. The deep sheltered water gives them perfect conditions to hide while they wait for the SC56. They seem to know their way around the Westervoe coastline, which suggests they have been in these waters before. I.C.E. has asked me to investigate some of the historical records in Breckwall Library. Apparently there is a documented sighting of a mermaid at the Point a hundred years ago. I want to find out if the sighting coincides with any curse activity at that time. Then we'll know for certain it was actually a Jellat.'

Archie considered telling Rufus about Ruby's Jellat but decided it would wait till later, along with the story of the black phantom and the strange mist as well as his sighting of Huigor. Right then he didn't want to talk, he just wanted to eat. He didn't want to admit to Rufus either that he was quickly going off the idea of exterminating the SC56.

Archie got forks and knives out of the drawer and salt and vinegar out of the cupboard.

'Double portions,' Rufus announced as he opened the wrapping, and everything that had happened that day was put to one side as Archie breathed in the warm aroma.

All conversation ceased as they began to tuck in and it wasn't until much later, when they were seated in front of the fire toasting marshmallows, that Archie told Rufus about Ruby's Jellat.

'She's got it in a tank in her bedroom. She caught it at the caves.'

Rufus sat back in surprise. 'What's she planning to do with a Jellat?'

Archie shrugged. 'It ate her terrapins. I don't think she really wants it any more. She said its singing gives her a headache.'

'If she can hear it, then she's susceptible to its influence! How was her general behaviour?'

'A bit odd. She told me her father was killed by a cursed lion in the jungle, but I checked with Miss Napier and she'd never heard of such a curse. Besides, lions don't live in the jungle.'

Rufus looked thoughtful. 'Are there any other surprises you've been keeping from me?'

Archie told him about the strange creature near the crossroads and the white mist that had come to his rescue and the suspended raindrops that showed him visions.

'What does it mean?' he asked.

'It means that by surviving the lightning strikes inside Huigor and the surge of energy that passed through Miss Napier's shoe, you have been left with exceptional talents,' Rufus explained. 'Tonight has proven that you have the ability to read Icegull breath, something the human eye is normally incapable of doing.'

'What do you mean, read Icegull breath?'

'The mist you walked into tonight was the breath of dying Icegulls. What we call the Mist of Knowledge. Each tiny drop of moisture holds a fragment of information. That's why Icegull breath makes perfect ink. It is a natural means of communication. Miss Napier writes the codicils, but the ink provides her with detailed information.'

'What has that got to do with me being able to read Icegull breath?' asked Archie.

'When the single drop of water fell from the ceiling on to your spine, it reacted with your force field, causing your senses to become heightened. It also left you with the rare gift of being able to read Icegull breath,' said Rufus.

'Why did the mist show me a crossed torch and dagger?'

'I don't know. But rest assured the meaning will become apparent to you when the time is right.'

Rufus handed Archie a toasted marshmallow. It was burnt on one side. Archie stared at the small black circle.

'And I saw Huigor tonight as well.'

Rufus almost dropped the toasting fork. 'Where?'

'In the school. We have a fungus on the classroom ceiling . . . well, we did have . . . It fell off. Huigor was hiding inside it.'

Rufus didn't appear surprised at this information. 'I saw his tracks up at the memorial. But what exactly did you see?'

'A shadow,' Archie told him. 'About the size of a rugby ball. It spun itself into a tornado shape in front of the fan heater Mr Petrie put in the classroom.'

'Don't worry about Huigor. He's still too weak to have any influence.' Rufus looked thoughtfully at Archie. 'When did you go into the school?'

Archie felt his cheeks burn. 'On my way home from Ruby's.'

Rufus continued to stare at him as he waited for more details.

'I wanted to look inside the art cupboard,' Archie explained. 'A couple of days ago I saw the shadow slip under the door.'

Rufus's response surprised him. 'Are you carrying any of the artefacts?'

Archie was so taken aback that he could only stutter, 'I . . . I have the key.'

Archie could tell Rufus was disappointed.

'The artefacts are not for everyday use,' Rufus gently reminded him. 'The I.C.E. Code of Practice stipulates they are for curse extermination only. Their power can be unpredictable and therefore dangerous. You must promise not to use any of them again until we're ready to deal with the SC56.'

Archie nodded and promised he would.

Rufus threw another log on to the fire and Archie caught sight of the old scar on his neck and the fresh red scratch next to it. It seemed like the perfect time to ask, 'How did you get the cut on the back of your neck?'

Rufus shrugged. 'Oh. Just being careless, I guess. It'll soon heal up.'

'No. I mean the old scar.'

Rufus stared thoughtfully at the sparks flying up the chimney. 'I'll tell you some other time.'

'Is it to do with a curse you exterminated?'

But Rufus was determined not to answer the question. He stood up and put the fireguard around the hearth.

'I'm tired and you must be tired too. Go to bed. Remember to keep the lights switched on overnight. Just a precaution.'

Archie did feel exhausted. It had been a long and eventful day, but with no school the following morning he would have another opportunity to question Rufus about his past. So he left his damp socks next to his wet shoes at the foot of the stairs and climbed up to his attic room. He was too tired to brush his teeth or even change into his pyjamas and he fell into bed fully clothed with the pebble tightly clutched in his hand.

Chapter Thirty-eight

Two thoughts occurred to Archie when he opened his eyes on Friday morning. The first was that his mother and father were coming home that day, which made him feel instantly happier. The second was how unusually quiet the room was. It had stopped raining and the Icegull breath was no longer dripping into the bucket. Archie felt an unease he couldn't explain, but which made him sit up and search under his quilt for the pebble. When he couldn't find it, there followed a moment or two of panic before he discovered it wedged down the back of his bed. He turned to look at the weatherscope and saw the glass had turned a deeper shade of blue overnight and the vibrating planets inside it were barely visible. That's when he decided to gather all the artefacts together.

The SC56 was closing in and he could sense its growing presence just as strongly as the weatherscope. Archie pulled the shoebox out from under his bed, along with an old rucksack, and carefully transferred the artefacts into it. When he picked up the dagger, he was hoping for the same sensation of bravery that had helped him exterminate Huigor. To his disappointment he felt only cold metal in his palm and a few static sparks. But with all the artefacts together in the bag he at least felt prepared for the battle ahead.

Archie was congratulating himself on being organised when he heard a seagull give a long soulful cry.

He hurried to the window, but as he swerved to avoid the bucket he noticed it was almost full of water. When he looked at it more closely, he saw his reflection was a rainbow of colours and his eyes in particular had the appearance of two bright jewels: a sapphire and an emerald.

'Mature Icegull breath,' he whispered, and his voice was filled with awe.

He dipped his hand into the water and then allowed it to run down over his fingers. It felt soft to the touch, like oil, except it wasn't greasy. His preoccupation with the Icegull breath was suddenly interrupted by the appearance of the herring gull coming in to land on the tree.

It settled itself on a branch and looked at him expectantly. Archie stared back and the gull continued to hold his gaze. Archie stood at the window and muttered, 'What do you want?'

The bird turned its head away to look out through

the branches towards the sea. Archie waited, feeling sure the gull would turn and look at him again. When it did, he was shocked by the soulful look in its eyes.

Archie repeated his question more urgently. 'What do you want? What are you trying to tell me?'

He wasn't prepared for what happened next. The gull opened its beak and threw back its head. Archie couldn't believe what he was hearing. Surely he was mistaken. He frantically tried to slide open the window but the wooden frame was swollen with the rain. He knocked on the glass and shouted, 'What did you say? What did you say?'

The bird continued to look at him with those sad unblinking eyes. Archie pressed his ear against the cold glass and waited, his heart thumping in anticipation. Then he heard the bird's strange squawking cry again and this time he was not mistaken.

'Saaaave Roooooooffffuuuuuuuus. Saaaave Roooooooffffuuuuuuuus.'

A cold, numbing chill crept over Archie's skin, making him shiver so that he was hardly aware of the bird spreading its wings and flying away, or that somebody was ringing the doorbell, over and over again.

Sid was standing on the doorstep. His bike was lying on the path. He stopped wiggling his tooth to announce, 'We've got an emergency.'

'What do you mean, an emergency?' Archie asked, as he searched the sky above Sid's head for the gull.

Sid gave a watery sniff. 'George and Ruby have gone out to the Point.'

'What!'

Raindrops were dripping from the tree on to Sid's head. 'Can I come in?' he asked.

Archie stood aside and Sid walked into the hall.

'How do you know George and Ruby are at the Point?' Archie wanted to know.

Sid kicked off his wellies. 'Ruby phoned to ask if I wanted to go with them.' He looked indignant. 'I hadn't even had my breakfast! And when I said we're not supposed to go out to the Point, she said I was "useless" and they were going anyway.'

Archie shut the front door and they walked upstairs to his room. Sid immediately noticed the bucket and the damp patch on the ceiling.

'We've got leaks in our house, too. There's been a flood warning as well.'

Archie was otherwise preoccupied. 'What time did Ruby phone?'

Sid sat down at Archie's computer and started loading Knight of the Five Tigers. 'Around nine, I think. What do you think we should do?'

There was only one answer to this question. 'I'm going to ask my Uncle Rufus.'

Sid looked worried. 'My mum says your Uncle Rufus is odd.' He registered Archie's offended expression. 'What I mean is . . . maybe we should ask . . .'

Archie was defiant. 'Rufus is not odd. He's an explorer. Wait here.'

'OK,' Sid told him. Then he made himself comfortable at the computer and began shooting tigers with flaming torches. He was so engrossed in the game that he didn't notice Archie creep back into the room and pick up the rucksack containing the artefacts. He couldn't risk Sid finding them.

Archie hurried down the stairs and into the kitchen. Without his parents, there were no mugs of tea cooling on the table, or crumbs around the toaster, or butter melting in the dish. There was no sign of Rufus either, although the TV was switched on. However, he had left a note on the kitchen table.

At the library. Back soon. Wait for me.
Rufus

Archie stood in the quiet of the kitchen trying to decide what to do. The weather report was beginning on the TV and, remembering what Sid had said about a high tide warning, he turned up the volume.

'. . . the equinox is bringing in these unsettled conditions,' the weather forecaster was saying. 'Heavy rain will persist in most areas and expect strong gusts of wind between showers. Be prepared for exceptionally high tides, too.' Archie stood looking at the screen, listening and waiting, and then she said it. 'Those of you in the Westervoe area are advised to get sandbags ready . . .'

Archie dashed into the corridor at the back of the house and got his bike. Then he pushed it back through the kitchen and out into the hallway. He put on his damp socks and shoes, grabbed his jacket from the peg and pulled on the rucksack. There was no time to lose. The SC56 was closing in and George and Ruby were out at the Point, possibly heading for the caves. He had to stop them.

He stood at the bottom of the stairs and shouted, 'Sid? Let's go.'

Sid came running down the stairs. 'Where are we going? Where's your Uncle Rufus? Isn't he coming?'

'Wait a minute.' Archie made a quick dash back into the kitchen. He found a pen in the fruit bowl under some mouldy bananas and added his own message to Rufus's note.

Gone out to the Point with Sid to look for George and Ruby.
P.S. the weather forecaster said to get the sandbags ready.
P.P.S. Got all the artefacts with me.

'Where are we going?' Sid asked as he followed Archie out of the house.

'We're going to the Point.'

Sid was unsure. 'On our own?'

Archie hesitated. 'Yes.'

'But we're not supposed to!'

'We won't go as far as the caves. We'll just see if we can catch up with George and Ruby and get them to turn back.'

Sid didn't look convinced as he followed Archie down the garden path. He would have preferred to stay and play on the computer than go out to the Point.

'What's in your rucksack?' he asked. But Archie was already racing down the hill and he had no choice but to give chase.

When they reached Ezekiel's cottage, they took a right turn on to a road that would take them out of the village and towards the Point.

Archie was cycling well ahead as they approached the crossroads. In the morning light and in the company of Sid, the prospect of seeing the black creature didn't seem so frightening, but he kept his eyes on the far distance and told himself to keep pedalling, which might have worked if Sid hadn't started shouting, 'Wait for me. Wait!'

Archie looked back over his shoulder. Sid was wobbling all over the road while trying to keep control of his bike. Archie braked and waited until Sid had regained control.

'What is it?' Archie asked.

Sid didn't answer. His skinny legs were pumping the pedals so fast they were almost a blur as he raced by, his eyes wide with terror.

Archie didn't waste any time. He had a pretty good idea what Sid had seen and he sped away after him. It was only when they reached the narrow road that would take them down to the Point that they stopped to catch their breath.

'I'm not going back that way,' Sid said between gasps.

'What did you see?' Archie asked.

'A face. In the ditch. Looking at me.'

'Whose face?'

Sid shook his head. 'It wasn't a person. It was an animal. Red eyes and a mane like a lion!' He scared himself just by talking about it, and quickly mounted the pedals and set off again.

They freewheeled down the hill, which gave Archie a good view of Moss Rock and a stretch of turbulent water beyond the Point called Thomson's Beard. This was where strong currents met. Perhaps it was the effect of the equinox, but Archie felt sure the white-tipped waves looked more turbulent than usual.

He turned his eyes to the shoreline, but there was no sign of George or Ruby, or anyone else for that matter.

At the bottom of the hill they braked heavily and swung on to a potholed track that ran along the top of the beach.

Archie kept his sights on the Point until they reached the end of the track and their way was barred by a wire fence hemming in a field of sheep. One of the sheep had managed to escape and they could see it up ahead, running along a narrow strip of grass at the edge of the rocks.

Archie and Sid dismounted their bikes and left them at the side of the track, then they walked down over huge boulders on to the sand.

'We'll go as far as the headland,' Archie decided. 'If there's still no sign of George or Ruby we'll turn back.'

It didn't take long before they were standing on the rocky headland where Archie had first heard the sound of distant marching. He didn't tell Sid that he could hear it now, except it sounded more like ten advancing regiments on the warpath.

'Why are you staring like that?' Sid asked.

'Like what?'

'Like you can hear something.'

'I was listening for Ruby or George.'

'I don't think we should go any further,' Sid decided. 'Maybe we should just shout and see if they shout back.'

Archie didn't think that was a practical idea. 'They won't hear us. We're not close enough.'

Sid looked at the sea. 'Is the tide coming in or going out?'

'Going out . . . I think.'

This news persuaded Sid to continue picking his way over the green slime covering the rocks, although most of the time he seemed to be crawling on all fours.

'I thought Ruby was quite nice the first day at school,' he told Archie. 'But now I'm not so sure.'

'What exactly did you overhear Mr Taylor and Mrs Merriman say about Ruby?' Archie asked.

Sid considered the question for a moment before recounting the incident.

'They were standing at the window watching Slaverin' Joe trying to fix the broken drainpipe. They didn't know I was in the classroom. Mrs Merriman said Ruby's dad had been killed on a secret service mission and now her mum thought it had something to do with Ruby's behaviour because she was acting oddly, like seeing things and having nightmares and stuff.' Sid picked up a long stalk of seaweed that looked like a lion's tail and began dragging it behind him.

'I've noticed other people acting oddly, too. I mean, look at George. I thought he was just jealous of you and Ruby being friends. He even told me he didn't like her. Now he's gone off with her. Maybe it's the full moon that's doing it. It can turn people odd, you know . . .' Sid gasped. 'Oh no!'

They had turned the corner of the headland. Neither had ever been that far before so the sight of the black rock rearing up beside them and the open ocean dipping and rising like a roller coaster was terrifying. They stood in silence taking in the scale of what they were seeing.

'I've never seen the sea roll around like that,' said Sid. 'I'm not staying here any longer!'

'Sssshh,' said Archie. He was listening for voices but all he could hear was the constant sound of marching over the waves hitting the rocks. He cupped his hands either side of his mouth and shouted. 'Geooooorge! Ruuuubbyyy!'

They waited for voices that never answered. Loose lumps of rock fell from the side of the cliff face and clattered on to the rocks close to where they stood. A gull squawked overhead. A cold chill blew in off the sea.

'They're not here,' Sid told him. 'I'm going back.'

Archie looked towards the caves. Was Huigor in there? Growing stronger as he waited for the SC56 to arrive?

'Don't try and go in,' Sid was pleading. 'If anything happens to you I won't be able to help.'

Archie looked at Sid as if he was mad. 'I'm not going in!'

He turned his attention back to the sea. The Glimpers had stopped marching and there were no

Jellats to be seen, yet Rufus had said they were congregating in large numbers. More loose rock fell and they looked up to see the escaped sheep standing at the edge of the rocks above the caves.

'Go away!' Sid shouted to it. His voice had the desired effect and the startled sheep turned, but the loose rock it had been standing on gave way and it stumbled. For a few moments its hind legs hung over the edge, desperately struggling to find a foothold.

'It's going to fall,' Sid said and sure enough the sheep slipped over the edge. They watched its thick body twist in mid-air and it gave one terrified bleat before falling headfirst into the deep water at the mouth of the cave. Bubbles rose up and broke the surface but the sheep didn't emerge again.

'That's odd,' Sid remarked. 'It must be trapped.' He took a step back as seawater rolled over the rocks close to where they stood. 'The tide's not going out. It's coming in!'

Overhead a gull began screeching and circling as if to warn them of the rising water and Archie recognised the distinctive line of black feathers beneath one wing.

Sid recognised it too and he scrambled over to where Archie stood. His hand was shielding his eyes from the gull.

'I don't think George and Ruby are here. I really don't.' He clung to Archie's arm. 'Let's go !'

'Don't grip me,' Archie told him. 'You'll make me slip.'

But the gull was swooping closer and Sid was tightening his grip. 'We shouldn't have come out here. Mr Taylor told us not to. We should have listened.'

While Sid shielded his eyes, Archie was looking towards the mouth of the cave. The water was rippling and stained red and he could see movement close to the surface. There was a sudden splash and the sheep's carcass was tossed out of the water and into the air. Parts of its fleece were hanging from its body and he could see its ribs where the meat had been ripped from the bone. A large tentacle reached up out of the sea, wrapped itself around the sheep's neck and pulled it underwater again.

Sid had seen it too. 'An octopus!' he shrieked. 'Run!'

A wave broke over the rocks, just missing them.

Sid tugged Archie's arm and then they were both falling and sliding on their backs towards the sea. Overhead the gull screeched and swooped.

Archie felt something grab the back of his jacket and he stopped sliding. He had been saved by his rucksack snagging on the rocks, but Sid was no longer beside him and he could hear screaming. Archie pulled himself up on to his knees to see Sid struggling in the water. He wasn't screaming any more and his head was barely above the surface. His terrified eyes were staring at

241

Archie and a strange sound was coming out of his mouth, as though he was trying to say something but couldn't.

'Hold on,' Archie shouted. 'I'm coming.'

But what was he to do? Sid was just out of reach, the sea was running fast and now a large clump of tentacles was heading straight for him.

Chapter Thirty-nine

All that was visible of Sid was his hands flailing in the water. The rest of his body was submerged in the sea. Archie lay down on his stomach and stretched his arm out, but Sid was still out of reach. In a last desperate attempt to save him, Archie looked for something to throw as a lifeline.

Close by the seagull was calling to him. Resting in its beak was the stalk of seaweed Sid had been dragging across the rocks. Archie grabbed hold of it and cast it towards Sid, whose head had just resurfaced. It took three frantic attempts before Archie felt Sid's grip on the stalk and pulled him to the side of the rocks.

'Don't let go,' Sid gasped as Archie held his arm. But then his throat gurgled and he gave a terrified scream. 'Something's beneath me! The octopus!' He began clawing at Archie's hands as he fought to get out of the water. 'Help me!' he spluttered. 'Don't let it eat me!'

But Archie didn't know how much longer he could

keep Sid afloat. His wet clothes and water-filled boots were weighing him down and sea water was already lapping around his mouth. The Jellat tentacles, too, were almost upon him. Archie turned and looked back over his shoulder, desperate for help, but even the gull was gone.

He heard a shrill scream and turned back to see a tentacle reach for Sid. Archie used the last of his strength to try and haul Sid clear, but he was in danger of being pulled into the water himself. The situation seemed hopeless when Sid's head and shoulders suddenly rose up out of the sea and then his arms and upper torso cleared the surface, too. In a wash of water he landed on the rocks, gasping and groaning.

Archie was left staring into the glistening eyes of a Glimper, whose enormous claws waved in the air. Beside it was the Jellat.

Archie scrambled away and pulled Sid to his feet. He was dragging him up to higher ground when he heard the sound of tentacles thrashing the water. He looked back and saw that the Glimper had the Jellat in its pincers and was ripping it to pieces. Sid was too shocked and cold to notice. His eyes had a glazed distant look to them as Archie helped pull off his boots and empty them of water. Then he draped his own coat around Sid's shoulders and they slowly made their way back across the rocks.

Beyond the Point, the empty beach stretched before them into the distance with not one solitary figure to call on for help. By the time Sid staggered over the boulders and crawled up on to the grassy track where they had left their bikes, he collapsed with exhaustion. Archie was wondering how to get him home, when over the sound of Sid's shivering and chattering teeth he heard an engine and then a motorbike with a sidecar was racing along the track towards them.

Archie could tell Rufus was angry because he didn't ask what had happened or whether they had been at the caves. He just handed Archie back his jacket, wrapped his own big waxed coat around Sid and lifted him into the sidecar. He gave Archie the spare helmet and told him to get on the back of the motorbike. The cycles would wait till later. Then they set off at speed.

Archie held on tight as the world whizzed by in a freezing blur. The sleeves of his jacket were wet and the back of his hands were scratched and stinging from Sid clawing at him. He was shaking too. If the Glimper hadn't thrown Sid clear of the water . . . He closed his eyes because he couldn't bear to imagine the Jellat eating Sid.

They raced past Ormleigh House and as they negotiated a bend in the narrow road they came upon a slow-moving tractor. Rufus braked heavily. Archie clung on as they swung out into the road and the sidecar mounted the grassy verge. There was a terrifying moment when Archie thought they would end up in the ditch but Rufus remained in control. He accelerated, overtook the tractor and pulled back over to the left-hand side of the road. The bike accelerated again and the grass verge became a smooth green blur of colour as they raced along. But then, from out of nowhere, a black creature was racing beside them with panther-like strides. Its body was long and thin, and its mane streamed out behind as it ran. Then a second black creature appeared and was racing along on the other side of the bike. Perhaps it was the speed at which they were travelling, but to Archie it had the appearance of a shadow rather than solid flesh and bone.

Archie glanced down at Sid, who had covered his head with Rufus's coat and was unaware of what was going on, which was just as well.

The creatures had overtaken them and were now criss-crossing in front of the motorbike, trying to force Rufus to crash, but he kept his nerve and accelerated again. The faster he drove, the closer the creatures darted in front of the bike.

Rufus now was driving far too quickly. Archie clung on as the bike braked heavily and he found himself leaning to the right as they sped around another bend. Up ahead were the village speed limit signs and as the bike raced towards them the two creatures dropped back. Archie looked over his shoulder and what he saw made the hairs on the back of his neck bristle. The two creatures blended into one and stood up on two legs, looking more human than animal, and walked into the ditch at the side of the road.

Chapter Forty

They were a curious sight as they sped through the village, Archie on the back of the bike clinging to Rufus and Sid huddled in the sidecar under Rufus's coat. The commotion brought people to shop doorways and windows, including Sid's mother, who wore a horrified expression as the bike came to an abrupt halt outside the house. She was standing ready at the open door, looking suspiciously at Rufus as he lifted a dripping wet Sid out of the sidecar, stepped over the sandbags and carried him into the hall.

'What happened?' she asked.

Rufus set Sid down. 'Better get him warm, and quickly. He fell into the sea at the Point.'

Sid's mother pulled off the waxed coat with a disapproving look and handed it to Rufus. Then she turned her attention to Sid.

'What were you doing out at the Point?' she asked, but Sid was too cold to reply.

'Looking for George and Ruby,' Archie told her.

She was now pulling off Sid's boots. 'And whose idea was it to go out there?'

'Mine,' said Archie.

Sid's mother stared at him. 'George and Ruby phoned here ten minutes ago and said they were sitting in the café if Sid wanted to join them. Nothing was mentioned about going out to the Point. Who in their right mind would be out there in weather like this?' She turned to Rufus. 'Certainly not *normal* people.'

She stood up and opened the front door. It was clear she wanted them to leave. Archie looked at Sid's shivering blue-tinged face and said, 'I hope you feel better soon.'

Sid managed a weak shivering smile that revealed an empty space where his slack tooth had fallen out.

Rufus and Archie said goodbye and walked outside. Seconds later the door was slammed shut behind them.

Rufus decided they might as well check out the café to make absolutely sure George and Ruby were safe, and have some breakfast at the same time. Archie agreed, because he could tell Rufus was still angry with him for going out to the Point. He also wanted to discuss the black creatures they'd just encountered, and apart from all that, he was absolutely starving. But there was something that couldn't wait any longer.

'I.C.E. has put out an SC56 warning. The weather

forecaster said people in the Westervoe area should get their sandbags ready. Does that mean the SC56 is about to strike?'

'What did my note say?' Rufus asked.

'Back soon and . . . to wait for you.'

'Exactly! I told you the other night not to take things into your own hands.' Rufus sighed. 'Put on your helmet.'

He kick-started the bike, revved the engine and they set off in the direction of the Harbour View Café watched by a small group of disapproving bystanders.

They parked across the road from the café and Archie could smell chips and sausages and bacon. The cat that usually sat in the doorway was up on the window sill well out of the way of the sandbags lining the doorstep.

The café was busy, with all the window tables taken up by customers looking out through the grimy glass towards the boats being rocked by the swell.

'Not even high tide yet,' Slaverin' Joe was saying as the sea crept closer to the top of the harbour wall.

Rufus walked up to the counter to place their order while Archie found a table. He noticed George and Ruby sitting at the back of the café in Slaverin' Joe's usual seat. Joe was staring at them, willing them to leave, but they continued to blow lazy bubbles through straws into their milkshakes.

Archie got up and walked over to their table. 'Have you been out to the Point this morning?' he asked.

'Why?' said Ruby.

'I've just come from there and there's a heavy sea rolling. I'd stay away if I was you.'

'So it's all right for you to go there?' said George. 'Was your bank robber uncle holding your hand?'

Ruby was curious. 'Your uncle's a bank robber?'

'No!'

'He's an explorer,' George sneered through another cold sore.

Archie had a sudden urge to pour the milkshake over George's head, but his hands and feet were tingling again and anyway he'd seen enough wet heads for one day.

'It was just a piece of advice,' he told them. 'Take it or leave it.'

He returned to his table just as Maggie set a plate of eggs, bacon, sausage and beans in front of him, and a glass of milk, too. Rufus had a glass of water.

Archie was starving but he wanted answers. He waited until Maggie was out of earshot before whispering, 'What kind of animal chased us? It had a separate shadow. They joined together and walked into the ditch on two legs. I saw it last night on the way home from Ruby's, and Sid saw it in the ditch on the way to the Point. What does it want with us?'

Rufus shook his head. 'It's not after you or Sid. It's called the Monstrum, and it's me it wants.'

'Why?'

Rufus lowered his voice. 'The Monstrum is a curse I broke a long time ago. It's become reactivated and is using the curse activity around Westervoe to grow in strength. It'll regain its full power if the SC56 hits.'

'Just like Huigor!'

Rufus nodded. 'You can't hide from curses once they're reactivated. They'll find you no matter where you are.'

'What kind of curse is the Monstrum?'

'I came across it one winter in a small Romanian village. The people talked of a black creature that prowled the houses at night, feeding on sickness and desperation. The weaker the villagers became, the stronger the creature grew. One night we gathered the villagers inside the courtyard of a nearby castle. We lit a huge fire and waited. Sure enough, a large black creature could be seen creeping around the stone walls. All we had to do then was catch it.'

'How did you do that?'

'The Icegulls froze it with their icy breath. Then we put it on a cart and took it up into the mountains and buried it. By spring the village had recovered. The Monstrum unfortunately survived the thaw. When it emerged, it could separate itself from its Shadow. That's what you saw today. It followed me around the world looking for revenge and caught up with me in the rain-forests of Brazil.'

Archie thought back to the vision he'd seen at I.C.E. when he'd shaken Miss Napier's hand.

'Did you exterminate the Monstrum in the rain-forest?'

Rufus nodded. 'I thought I had seen the last of it. But here it is again, thanks to the SC56.'

'How will the Monstrum take its revenge on you?' Archie asked.

'The Shadow will pass into my body and slowly drain me of life. The Monstrum has a long memory, particularly when it comes to settling old scores. Where it cannot take revenge on an adversary, for instance if he or she is already dead, then it will target a blood relative.'

'It was the Monstrum Shadow that got into the bank, wasn't it?' asked Archie. 'That's what you meant when you said whatever took the pebble wasn't human.'

Rufus nodded. 'The herring gull confirmed exactly what I suspected. The Shadow slipped in under the door. It was able to manipulate the locks to my safe and strongbox. Then it was just a case of rolling the pebble out through a rat tunnel. Fortunately, the gull was waiting outside and managed to snatch it back before the Monstrum got a hold of it.'

'The Shadow got into I.C.E., too. I saw it on the stairs.'

Rufus nodded. 'The Monstrum wants the pebbles, to stop us breaking curse activity for ever. And it wants me!' He rubbed his hands over his face. 'Enough questions. Eat your breakfast!'

Archie began to eat so quickly that Rufus had to tell him to slow down. Then he asked, 'So what happened at the Point?'

Archie looked at the deep scratches on his hands.

'Sid slipped on the rocks at the caves and fell in. A Glimper fished him out.'

Rufus rested his arms on the table and leaned closer.

'See anything else?'

'Just one big Jellat. It ate a live sheep. It almost got Sid.' He couldn't bring himself to describe the details so instead he asked, 'Did you find anything out at the library?'

Rufus nodded. 'The date of a mermaid sighting and a ship sinking coincided. I spoke to I.C.E. and they believe a Jellat colony was responsible for the disappearance of a schooner a hundred years ago.' Rufus dipped his finger into his glass of water and spun it round and round to create a whirlpool. 'That's what Jellats do with their tentacles to create whirlpools. They use this technique to drag down into the sea anything too heavy to manhandle, such as boats. Or to store fresh prey until it's ready to eat.'

Archie grimaced.

'The one thing we have in our favour,' Rufus was now saying, 'is they won't feed close to the SC56 striking. A full stomach would slow them down.'

Archie wasn't sure he wanted to hear any more. Fortunately, Rufus changed the subject.

'I.C.E. told me something about herring gulls today. They found a reference in their archives describing the gulls as good-natured though not playful, and reliable and efficient workers.' Rufus smiled. 'But we knew that anyway.'

Archie smiled back but decided against telling Rufus what the gull had said that morning outside his bedroom window. He didn't see any point in adding to his worries. Instead he began to eat the last sausage while thinking over everything Rufus had just told him, particularly about the Monstrum.

'Ruby said her father was killed by a black lion,' he told Rufus. 'But maybe she got it wrong. Maybe it was a creature that looked like a lion. The Monstrum kind of looks like a black lion, doesn't it?' Rufus didn't reply so Archie continued. 'The mane and the tail definitely make it look like a lion. And maybe her father wasn't killed in the jungle at all. Maybe it was in a rainforest. Maybe the Monstrum killed her father in the Brazilian rainforest and you were there, too.'

Rufus stared at Archie. 'Your purpose right now is to focus on the SC56. Anything else can wait.'

But Archie wasn't finished. 'You said the Monstrum will go after people of the same family. Is Ruby in danger? Should I warn her?'

This was a question Rufus was prepared to answer. 'The Monstrum is after me.' He pointed to the fresh scratch on the back of his neck. 'It tasted my blood. It has my scent. Ruby is safe as long as it's hunting me . . .'

'But what if it kills you?'

'We have to stay focused and make sure that doesn't happen.'

Archie looked towards the grimy windows. 'I wish the SC56 would just hurry up and get here so I can get on with exterminating it.'

'It's closer than you think. When I was on the phone to I.C.E., I also spoke to Miss Napier. She predicts the SC56 will strike at high tide in the powerful colliding currents of Thomson's Beard.' He looked at his watch. 'That gives us an hour and a half.'

Archie's breakfast began to churn around in his stomach.

Rufus registered his nervousness. 'You showed enormous courage in exterminating Huigor, but today you risked Sid's life as well as your own. You have to listen to experienced curse exterminators, like myself, and show respect for knowledge that hasn't come easy. You can't take unnecessary risks where other people are concerned –'

'I was trying to save George and Ruby –'

'They weren't even at the Point! Do you remember what I said? Don't panic, keep a clear head and –'

'– make a sound judgment,' Archie told him.

Rufus's voice turned gentle. 'Don't confuse courage with recklessness.' He looked again at his watch. 'OK. Let's go.' He pushed back his chair and a fork clattered to the floor. They realised the café had gone quiet, as if everyone had been trying to eavesdrop on their conversation. Archie was also aware of being watched as he followed Rufus out of the café. When he came to close the door, it was pulled open again.

Ruby stood in the doorway holding his rucksack. 'You forgot this.'

He had been so engrossed in his conversation with Rufus that he had forgotten all about the artefacts. He couldn't hide his gratitude as he accepted the rucksack.

'Thank you. Thank you *very* much. There are some really important things inside it . . .'

But Ruby was thinking of something other than the rucksack.

'I'm not a liar,' she said softly. She appeared perfectly calm in contrast to her hysterical mood the day before.

'I know you're not a liar,' he told her. 'I'm sorry I didn't believe what happened to your father. Or that you have a picture of a Jellat.'

A voice from inside the café shouted, 'Close that door. It's freezing in here!'

Ruby walked outside with him and shut the door. 'My Jellat's dead.'

'How?' he asked.

'My mother threw it on the compost heap. She thought it was rotting seaweed.' She shrugged. 'At least I don't have to listen to that horrible singing any more. My headaches have gone, too.' Ruby looked back through the café door window and, seeing George staring at them, quickly turned to Archie. 'Do you want to come for tea tonight? My unicycle arrived from London this morning. We could ride it in the corridors at Ormleigh House. Should be fun.'

Archie would have loved to try out the unicycle, but it wouldn't be that afternoon. 'I've got something to do,' he told her. 'I'm not sure how long it'll take.' He saw Ruby's disappointment and added, 'But I'll come round sometime soon.' This made her instantly cheer up.

He would have liked to warn her about the Monstrum, but since he wasn't sure if it went against the I.C.E. code of practice, he chose to say, 'The weather forecast isn't good. Go home until after high tide.' As an afterthought he added, 'And keep the lights on.'

Ruby looked surprised at this strange request but said she would. She was making her way back inside the café to get her jacket when a thought crossed Archie's mind.

'Who did your father work for before he died?'

'Nobody you would have heard of. A small specialist organisation.' She looked back over her shoulder before closing the door. 'Called I.C.E.'

Archie slung the rucksack over his shoulder and crossed the road to where Rufus was getting his coat out of the sidecar.

'We'll take Ezekiel's boat out,' Rufus told him, as he pulled on the coat. 'Try and get as near as possible to Thomson's Beard.'

Perhaps it was the damp chilly air, but Archie felt shivers on his spine. He thought he heard the sound of running paws on the ground and panting breath. He spun round, but apart from the cat on the café window sill, arching its back and spitting, and a dog barking in the distance, there were no other animals to be seen.

'Are you ready?' Rufus asked him.

Archie looked out on to the rolling grey sea. The vision of the future he'd seen through the telescope at I.C.E. had been of Rufus looking over the side of a small boat that was being tossed by a treacherous swell. There had been no sign of himself aboard that boat, in which case had the telescope been showing him he would not survive the SC56?

Chapter Forty-one

Ezekiel's boat was called the *Ola* and it was moored at the far end of the pier. Normally, Archie and Rufus would have had to climb down a metal ladder set into the harbour wall to reach the deck, but the unusually high tide had raised the hull well above the pier and the boat was rearing up out of the water like a restless horse.

Archie put on a life vest while Rufus cast off the ropes. There was no one to watch them set sail apart from a couple of seagulls that followed the boat as far as the harbour mouth, swooping and calling as if warning them to turn back.

Once outside the relative shelter of the bay the gulls turned and Archie watched them head towards Westervoe. A part of him wanted to fly back with them. He felt unnerved by the great expanse of rolling sea and he was sure the boat was too small and vulnerable to negotiate the stormy conditions.

Shivers, too, were rippling up and down his spine and a tingling sensation was spreading through his fingers. He was feeling the strength of curse energy he couldn't see but knew to be close by. This was confirmed by the appearance of what looked like a clump of seaweed that kept pace with the boat.

Archie kept his eyes on the tangle of tentacles until they rounded the first headland and the tall frame of the unlit beacon came into view. He was so entranced by the unpredictable motion of the waves swirling around the metal legs that by the time he turned to look back at the clump of tentacles it had disappeared.

He walked unsteadily across the rocking deck and into the wheelhouse. Rufus was looking through a pair of binoculars at the sea up ahead.

'We're being followed by Jellats,' Archie told him.

But Rufus was more concerned with the condition of the sea. He pointed to chaotic white-tipped waves beyond the Point.

'Thomson's Beard doesn't look too good. I think we should wait here while I assess the situation.'

Rufus cut the engine and dropped the anchor. Apart from the sea slapping against the boat and the creak of wood, it was eerily quiet.

The air had turned colder too, and occasional heavy spots of rain hit the deck. There were no more gulls crying overhead, not even a sea breeze blowing in

Archie's ears, just the up and down motion of the sea. There was no sound of an advancing army either.

'Why aren't the Glimpers marching?' he asked.

'Shhhh!' Rufus told him. 'Listen!'

Archie listened. He could hear the distant moan of a boat engine, or perhaps an aeroplane, but then he realised the sound was not mechanical but animal.

'Hold on!' Rufus warned as the sea split open and something large and grey loomed up out of the water either side of them. Archie's first thought was that they were about to be attacked by serpents again but Rufus shouted, 'Whales!'

A tail lashed the surface and three more huge grey bodies cut through the water, so close that the wash rocked the boat and Archie caught the scent of their breath.

'They're heading inland,' Rufus told him. 'The SC56 must be confusing them.'

Archie watched the whales swim through the swollen sea that was as black and grey as the sky. He could no longer see the horizon. The hairs on the back of his neck were bristling and the tingling sensation spreading through his fingers and toes was growing stronger. He sensed something was about to happen, when a long tentacle suddenly shot up out of the water next to the boat and hovered above the deck.

'Take cover in the wheelhouse,' Rufus told him, as

the sea turned a murky shade of brown and green. More and more tentacles were rising to the surface and crawling up the sides of the boat, camouflaging it to look like a rock.

'Let's get out of here,' Rufus said, but when he went to pull up the anchor he found it weighed down. He tried to start the engine but Jellats had jammed the rudder too.

Rufus was trying to decide what to do when the boat began to move of its own accord, and he could only watch helplessly as they were pulled through the sea at speed. Rufus joined Archie in the wheelhouse and pulled the door shut just as a heavy tentacle slapped against the window.

'Where are they taking us?' Archie wanted to know.

Rufus peered out through a corner of the window that wasn't already covered in sea spray. 'Looks like we're heading for the caves.'

Archie didn't like the sound of Rufus's prediction. 'But you said Jellats won't feed close to the SC56 approaching?'

Rufus nodded. 'They won't. I'd say we're going to be the Jellats' late lunch.'

Archie looked on to the swirling sea. It was the kind of sea that swallowed you up, took your breath away and didn't let you go. He couldn't swim very well, but what did it matter when the Jellats would catch him before he hit the water?

'What are we going to do?' he asked.

'No idea,' Rufus replied as the rocks loomed closer. 'Any suggestions?'

Archie reached inside the rucksack and grasped the dagger handle. He raised the blade above his head in an act of defiance but, disappointingly, he felt no ripple of bravery. He switched on the torch and a pale yellow glow lit up the underside of a large tentacle that was crawling over the wheelhouse window.

'Why aren't the artefacts activated? Why aren't they helping us?' he asked.

'Helping us, Archie? Or just doing it for us. How about calling on the power of the artefacts?'

'I didn't ask for their help when I battled Huigor.'

'Yes, you did. You allowed your instinct and intellect to guide you. Try and do the same thing now.' Rufus peered out through a small gap in the window. 'Preferably before we get dragged into the caves.'

Rufus grabbed the wheel and, using all his strength, tried to regain control of the rudder, but it was still stuck fast. Archie, meantime, was looking at the artefacts, trying to remember what each one was capable of. He pulled the flute from the rucksack and blew into it until he had no breath left. Still nothing happened and he gasped, 'The Icegulls are supposed to help when I play the flute.'

'Not if they're regenerating,' Rufus reminded him. 'Try again.'

Archie put the flute to his lips and blew. The tentacle that had been lying across the window flicked up and fell back into the sea.

Rufus opened the wheelhouse door very slightly and peered around the door frame. 'They're pulling away from the sides of the boat, too.' But it wasn't all good news. The boat was so close to the rocks they could almost reach out and touch them.

A loud thud rocked the underside of the hull and the bow was thrown up out of the water. Rufus and Archie fell to the wheelhouse floor.

'We've run aground,' Rufus said as he scrambled to his feet. 'If there's a hole in the hull, we're done for.' He staggered out on to the deck, and keeping hold of the handrail he checked for signs of damage. As far as he could see, they weren't taking on water. They had been thrown clear of the rocks, too, yet something solid was still knocking against the underside of the boat.

Archie pulled on his rucksack and stood at the wheelhouse door. 'The boat is turning,' he told Rufus. 'We're saved.'

Rufus made his way over to where Archie was standing. 'When you were blowing the flute, what thoughts were going through your head?'

'I called on the Glimper army to defend us against

the Jellats' attack.'

'Good. We can now see the results of intelligent and specific thinking. You've rallied the Glimpers. Let's hope they can take control of the boat and get us out to Thomson's Beard before the SC56 strikes.'

They looked out on a swirling frenzy of tentacles, small whirlpools and air bubbles. Gigantic claws were rising up out of the sea, clutching jelly bodies that were disintegrating into brown frothy slime.

Archie clung to the handrail as the boat pitched and rolled its way through the battle.

One minute the Jellats would congregate at the side of the boat and attempt to roll it over, the next a line of defending Glimpers would right them again. But still the Jellats kept coming, as though the sea was full of them right down to the ocean bed.

As they watched the battle unfold it was becoming clear that the Glimpers were outnumbered by the mass of tentacles.

'Things just aren't going our way, are they?' Rufus sighed as he pointed towards the towering structure of the beacon. Archie was no seaman but even he could tell they were heading towards the swirling water around the metal legs. With the Glimpers struggling to take control of the boat from the Jellats, Rufus pulled Archie back into the wheelhouse.

'Brace yourself,' he said as the boat was finally

caught in the water eddying around the beacon.

The vessel was thrown into a spin, the helm collided with one of the metal legs and they were pulled beneath the towering structure. The black metal frame straddled the boat like a strange water monster, creating an unnatural darkness inside the wheelhouse. Rufus held on to Archie as the boat began to spin again, but this time it turned only a hundred and eighty degrees before coming to a halt.

Rufus opened the wheelhouse door and looked over the side of the boat. There was no damage. What troubled him were the telltale yellow lights he could see in the water.

'The Jellats have attached us to the beacon leg. But why?'

'That's why,' Archie told him. He was pointing to a whirlpool forming close to the boat. 'They're going to suck us down into the sea.'

But Rufus wasn't looking at the whirlpool. His eyes were fixed on the back of the boat. 'Give me your pebble. Quickly!'

Archie pulled the pebble from his pocket and watched as Rufus placed it in his palm along with his own pebble, cupped his hands together and rattled the stones. When he opened his hands, the stones were vibrating and the arrows were pointing at one another.

'If we get separated, the arrow will show you which

direction to find me. Clasp it tightly and it'll give out a glowing light. Put it in your pocket. Keep it safe.'

Archie didn't like what he was hearing. 'What do you mean, if we get separated?' He thought back to Rufus jumping out of the plane and leaving him to the serpents. 'Where are you going this time?'

'It's here,' Rufus simply said.

Archie looked out on to the terrifying sea, expecting to see the SC56, but a low growl from the stern of the boat made him turn. Two large red eyes were peering from behind a stack of creels, then a black creature, half man and half lion, crawled out and bared its long yellow fangs.

'It must have crept on board at the harbour,' Rufus said.

Archie pointed the torch at the Monstrum and pressed the green button. There was no strong white burning light, just a regular yellow glow, but it was strong enough to startle the Monstrum. It leapt from the boat on to the beacon leg and climbed it with the ease of a cat. It perched itself like a vulture in front of the unlit lamp with its long mane blowing around its glowing red eyes. It gave Archie only a cursory glance before it gave a howl that sounded like a cruel laugh as it called to its Shadow. A long black shape crawled out from behind the creels and, unaffected by the motion of the boat, stood up on its hind legs to tower over them.

Archie shone the torch into its face and the glow lit up lifeless black holes that were its eyes. He was so mesmerised by this apparition that he was unaware of a large tentacle rising up out of the sea next to the boat until it had whipped itself around his waist. He let out a cry of surprise, but there was no time to grab Rufus's outstretched hand before he was lifted up and pulled over the side.

Chapter Forty-two

The Jellat tentacle tightly wrapped around Archie's stomach was squeezing the air from his lungs. He was being held upside down, too, and swung through the air so that the beacon appeared to dance back and forth through the turbulent sea. Then he was flicked upright and he found himself facing the boat.

He could see Rufus, trapped against the wheelhouse wall, and he caught a glimpse of the Monstrum Shadow advancing on him, before the tentacle was on the move again.

This time, Archie was heading straight towards one of the beacon legs. He stretched his arms out to protect himself from the impact and realised he was still holding the torch. It was welded to his palm just as his hands had been welded to the controls of the plane when the serpents had struck.

He raised his knees up and using the soles of his shoes he cushioned the impact as he was thrown against the beacon. His free hand reached for a clump of seaweed that was attached to the structure and, using it to anchor himself, twisted round and aimed the torch. To his dismay the beam of light failed to reach the Shadow as it prepared to attack Rufus, its huge gaping mouth stretching towards him.

This time Archie kept his finger pressed down hard on the green button as he called on the power of the artefacts. 'Save Rufus!' he shouted.

The torch jolted in his hand and a beam of hot white light shot out. At the same time a wave broke against the beacon, showering him in icy spray. Archie kept his finger pressed on the button. His entire body shuddered violently, his limbs went into spasm and the world turned a brilliant shimmering white. He felt as if he was being shaken out of his skin. It was the same sensation he had experienced inside the aeroplane when he had killed the serpents.

Jagged white light was racing up the metal supports of the beacon and in a shower of sparks the lamp burst into a blaze of dazzling light. The Monstrum appeared out of the glare and began to search frantically for somewhere to hide, but with no dark corner to crawl into, it gave a terrified howl and leapt towards the boat.

The Shadow, too, had pulled back from Rufus and was crouched and waiting. The moment the Monstrum landed on the deck, the Shadow crawled inside it with a savagery that made the Monstrum twist and howl.

Rufus had positioned himself at the bow of the boat, well away from the powerful torch beam. He watched as the Monstrum ran blindly back and forth across the deck, looking for a place to hide.

When the boat pitched violently, Archie lost sight of the Monstrum, but then the glare from the beacon picked up a familiar shape in the water. A long black limb was reaching up, searching for something to cling to, when it was caught by the spinning water and sucked down into the whirlpool.

Archie heard Rufus shout, 'Switch off the torch!'

He pressed the blue button and the white shimmering light disappeared. The beacon lamp flickered and died too. The boat swung close to Archie, and Rufus's outstretched hand was almost within touching distance, but the Jellat was shaking violently. A group of Glimpers were slicing through its tentacles with the ease of a sharp sword.

Archie let go of the clump of seaweed and reached once more for Rufus. There was a brief moment when their hands touched before the dying Jellat threw its tentacles into the air and Archie was tossed aside.

He heard Rufus shouting his name. He was aware of a spinning circle of yellow eyes beneath him, watching and waiting. His feet hit the icy water and the shock took his breath away. Tentacles shot up around him, keeping the Glimpers at bay, and through the confused sea he caught one last glimpse of Rufus. He was leaning over the side of the boat, reaching for him, just as Archie'd seen him do through the telescope at I.C.E.

But there was no rescue for Archie this time. The sea took over and he was sucked down into the Jellats' whirlpool.

Chapter Forty-three

One moment Archie was falling feet first inside the whirlpool, the next he was upside down and spinning, yet all the time he kept a tight hold of the torch.

He was now being sucked so fast through the whirlpool that all he could see was the blur of Jellat lights. He had no idea how far he had travelled when the tunnel began to narrow and he was no longer spinning. Splashes of water began to fall on to his head and he heard a sound like a long intake of breath. Then the sea closed in and deep icy water was swirling around him.

Panic started to rise but he remembered the life-saving tips they had been given at school, keeping your arms by your sides and kicking your legs. He was trying to do all these things when he found himself being pushed upwards so fast the water thundered in his ears. His head cleared the surface, but still he kept rising, until he was ejected by a waterspout at the top of the whirlpool. He couldn't tell where he was because of the darkness, but nearby he could hear the splash of water. He switched on the torch and discovered he was in a water-filled cave surrounded by fish going nowhere, trapped, just as he was: part of the Jellats' live stock of food for a post-SC56 feast. He pulled himself on to a narrow ledge and shone the torch along the walls. A startled seal slid into the water amid the frantic fish.

As far as Archie could make out, the cave narrowed into a channel and the ledge he was sitting on ran the full length of it. His spirits were further lifted by the sight of faint rays of daylight deep inside the channel, which surely meant he had an escape route. But first he had to let Rufus know he was still alive.

He pulled the pebble from his pocket and shook it in his cupped hands. It began to vibrate and the arrow-head pointed towards the daylight.

Archie returned the pebble to his pocket, wedged the torch into the belt of his jeans and, with the glow lighting up the wall, was able to find finger-grips. He began to make his way along the ledge, but his progress was slow. His wet clothes and shoes made it difficult to move and his chilled fingers were barely able to keep a hold of the rock. He couldn't tell if it was the bitter cold that was sending shivers up and down his spine or curse activity. Had the Monstrum also survived the whirlpool, and was it in the cave with him? Or was it Huigor he was sensing, waiting for him in the shadows up ahead?

He had other concerns too. The sea level in the cave was rising, and occasionally he could feel strong vibrations through the rock, which told him the SC56 was closing in. His resolve was further tested when the ledge narrowed to just a few centimetres and he had to balance on the tips of his shoes. Small rocks, too, were falling from the ceiling and narrowly missing his head, but the glimmer of daylight from just around the corner told him he would soon be free.

He emerged from the bend in the rock full of optimism only to find he had reached a dead end. The daylight he had so wanted to see was in fact pouring over the top of a sheer wall stretching far above him. With no other way out and the water now lapping at his heels, he had no choice but to start climbing.

He focused on finding gaps in the rock rather than worrying about the rapidly rising water, climbing slowly but steadily, keeping his sights on the daylight that was growing stronger as he neared the summit. By the time he found his final foothold he could hardly contain his relief and he eagerly peered over the top of the wall. Before him was a wide cavern of black rock and through a gaping hole in the ceiling he could see the sky.

Archie almost wept with disappointment as he looked up at the curved and impossibly high ceiling. With no means of escape and no chance of rescue, how was he to exterminate the SC56?

Chapter Forty-four

Archie could only stare in dismay at what confronted him. The one bit of comfort he could take from this new prison was that he now had daylight, but his plight was almost too much to bear. He was trapped inside a cavern that would flood once the sea poured over the wall he had just climbed.

He shivered from the cold and the uselessness of his situation. If he could just warm up, he felt sure he would be able to think more clearly.

Archie pulled the torch from his belt and pointed it at a shallow pool. He pressed the button and hot white light stirred up the water. When steam began to rise, he switched the torch off, dipped his fingers into the water and warmth spread up into his arms and settled in his chest.

He removed his rucksack, life vest and jacket, pulled off his soggy trainers and socks and slipped his feet into the pool. As his shivering body started to thaw, he began to consider his position.

The only help available to him was from the arte-facts. But what good was a key when there were no doors to unlock; or goggles inside a cavern that had no horizon. He was so preoccupied that he was unaware of a movement on the rock beside him. It was only when the pebble rolled over and came to rest next to his hand that he realised it was vibrating and the arrow was pointing to his left. Somewhere, beyond the thick walls of the cavern, Rufus was alive and searching for him.

Archie called out but no voice came back.

He pulled his feet out of the pool and discovered the rock around one edge was hot beneath his toes. When he came to put his socks on, he found they had already started to dry out and steam was rising from his clothes. He felt exhilarated by the deep warmth in his chest and his eyes sparkled as if he could see everything more clearly. He took a long intake of air and as his lungs filled he discovered he was in no hurry to exhale. His breathing had slowed right down. He returned the pebble to his trouser pocket, slipped the torch into his belt, and was reaching for the rucksack when a dark shadow fell across the pool.

Archie spun round. There behind him, hovering above the ground and spinning slowly, was a column of shadow and dust.

In one swift movement he grabbed the torch and

keeping his finger pressed down hard on the button he fired, blasting Huigor into a cloud of black dust that disappeared in a gust of wind. All Archie's senses were now on high alert.

When small stones fell from the ceiling, he looked up to see a blanket of shadow ripple along the walls. Archie fired the torch again. This time he kept his finger on the button until a loud crack echoed through the cave. High above him, a huge slab of rock had become dislodged by the force from the torch, and was hanging at a precarious angle, ready to topple over.

Archie picked up the rucksack and hurried towards the shelter of a narrow crevasse. He squeezed inside, covered his head with his arms and waited. And waited. But there was no sound of collapsing rock.

He cautiously edged to the entrance of the crevasse and peered round the corner. Looking back at him was a large black eye. The shock made Archie drop the torch. There wasn't time to pick it up before Huigor was swirling around his head, blinding him with choking dust. Archie got down on to his hands and knees and was fumbling around on the ground, searching for the torch, when Huigor roared and spun out of sight. The air cleared to reveal the Monstrum hauling itself over the wall and into the cavern. Its bedraggled hair hung in long wet strands and bits of Jellat tentacles were embedded in its matted mane, but it had lost none of the fire in its red eyes. They were looking up at Huigor as he delivered Archie's scent on a cold gust of wind.

Archie squeezed back into the crevasse as the Monstrum sniffed the air and began to search for him. He listened to its huge wet feet slap against the rock as it prowled the cavern, drawing closer all the time. He hardly dared breathe. And then it walked into view. Archie pushed further into the crevasse and the rucksack scraped against the stone.

The Monstrum stopped and turned its head to look directly at where Archie was hiding. It gave a low threatening growl and stood up on its hind legs.

Archie's hand was shaking as he pointed the torch. 'Keep a clear head,' he told himself as the lumbering body advanced to fill the space outside the crevasse.

Archie intended to wait until the Monstrum was close enough to take the full force of the torch beam. His finger was poised ready on the button but something was moving over his feet. He glanced down and a snake of dust and shadows raised its head. Huigor's distorted face was looking up at him.

Archie's brief moment of distraction had left him open to attack. The Monstrum lunged with a savage growl, its breath thick with the stench of decay. Saliva was dripping from its yellow fangs and its unblinking red eyes stared out from a head too large to enter the narrow crevasse. Archie fired the torch but the Monstrum was already reaching for him and he gave a cry of pain as a claw punctured his leg.

Huigor rose up but Archie kept his nerve. Through the choking dust he continued to direct the torch flare at the Monstrum until its growling was replaced with an agonised howl. Its head jerked violently backwards and it fell to the ground, but Archie kept up the pressure, forcing the disorientated beast to crawl beneath the overhang of loose rock. He swung the torch beam on to the huge slab of stone and it came crashing down with a force that shook the cavern.

Archie covered his eyes until he heard the last falling rock settle. When he peered out, Huigor was gone and all that was visible of the Monstrum was an arm protruding from under the pile of rocks.

Archie looked down at the blood seeping from the wound at the top of his leg, but his distress was for the hole in his jeans where the Monstrum had ripped the pebble from his pocket.

He walked over to where the creature lay and kicked the lifeless arm. It flopped over and he could see the paw was tightly clenched. Rather than touch the grotesque limb, he took the dagger from the rucksack and prised open the paw. To his disgust, he saw that the skin on its palm was thick and calloused. It had webbed fingers and long curved claws, one of which was stained with blood. But there was no pebble to be seen.

Archie carefully examined the ground. If the pebble was lying beneath the fallen rocks, then he had no way of retrieving it. Professor Himes had said to guard it with his life and now he had lost it before the SC56 had even struck. He was failing as a curse exterminator at every turn, and as if to remind him how close the SC56 was, a strong tremor rocked the cavern and the sea finally began flowing over the wall.

Archie looked up through the hole in the ceiling to a sky that was grey and threatening. A cold chill blew through the cavern and a whispering laugh echoed along the walls. He couldn't tell where it was coming from until a part of the wall took on the appearance of a face. It had one eye and a contorted mouth that opened to whisper, '*I am weak but my strength grows.*'

Archie crouched down behind the pile of fallen rock as Huigor rippled down the wall and drifted into the centre of the cavern. There he hovered above the ground and spun himself into a small tornado.

Faster and faster he turned, growing stronger with each rotation. Archie held on to a boulder as the wind raced around the cavern, scattering stones and blowing the rucksack into a corner.

'*When my power is restored, I will return,*' Huigor warned.

Then, making a sound like a rocket taking off,

Huigor flew out through the hole in the ceiling and disappeared.

The force of the wind had dislodged a boulder from the stack and Archie found himself looking down into the Monstrum's face. Its red unblinking eyes were staring up at him in a way that he couldn't tell if it was alive or dead.

He picked up a rock, took aim and was ready to strike when his arm was pushed aside in a flurry of feathers and beating wings. The herring gull landed on the Monstrum's head and immediately pushed its beak into the right eye socket. It pulled out the eyeball, tossed it aside and plunged its beak in again. This time it found what it was looking for. In its beak was the pebble, and after dipping it in the shallow pool, the gull dropped it into Archie's waiting hand. The whole operation had taken less than thirty seconds.

Having the pebble back was good news, but sea water was now lapping close to where Archie stood.

'Is there a way out?' he asked the gull.

The bird took off and landed on a ledge that had been created by the rock fall. Behind it Archie could see an opening.

'Find Rufus. Tell him I'm here.' His voice reverberated around the cavern as he shouted, 'Hurry!'

Archie put the pebble in his trouser pocket, retrieved his rucksack and tucked the torch into his belt. He was climbing up towards the opening when the sea finally flooded the cavern. By the time he reached the safety of the ledge the water was halfway up the wall. Beyond the opening he could see a labyrinth of passages. But which one should he take?

Archie opened the rucksack and took out the stopwatch. He pinned it to his jumper, clicked the button on the top and said, 'Let the hands show me the way.' A narrow ribbon of red light appeared on the ground at his feet and ran into one of the passages. Archie raised his fist in triumph and then quickly set about pulling the goggles on over his eyes. He tucked the dagger into his belt and with the torch in his hand, ready to use, he took his first cautious steps into the dark.

The red trail twisted and turned in a passage that was just wide enough for Archie to squeeze through. Sometimes he had to climb up over jagged rocks, other times he had to slide down steep ridges. All the time he could hear the rumble and roar of the SC56. Occassionally he saw shadows. Sometimes they were his own, other times he wasn't so sure, and then he began to imagine the Monstrum had freed itself and was following him.

All his senses were primed so that when two red eyes appeared in front of him his finger was ready to activate the torch.

'Don't shoot,' said a voice. 'It's me!'

Archie lowered the torch and there before him was Rufus, wet and cold, but alive. His eyes were bathed in the glow from the red trail that had stopped directly at his feet. Archie couldn't hide his relief.

'How did you get here?'

'Got your message from the herring gull. Decided to take a trip in the whirlpool for myself. Very interesting. It split into three funnels. Fortunately, I didn't end up with the Monstrum for company.'

'The Monstrum's dead! You're saved!' Archie told him. 'It's buried under a pile of rocks. But I think Huigor's gone to meet the SC56.'

A strong tremor rocked the ground beneath them. Rufus looked worried. 'We've got to get out of here. The tunnels are flooding. Some of them have already collapsed. We don't have long.'

They said no more, saving their energy instead for following the fast-moving red trail that led them to a narrow channel of water.

'There's our transport!' Rufus said as a couple of large Glimpers broke the surface.

They climbed aboard and the red trail faded, leaving them in the claustrophobic darkness of the channel. They travelled in wary silence. Occasionally Archie felt movement on his face, but he could see nothing as he looked back into the darkness. Rufus appeared uneasy too.

The channel narrowed, forcing them to travel in single file with Archie's Glimper leading the way. The water level continued to rise and a strong swell slapped the sides of the channel. Rufus dipped his head to avoid hitting it against the ceiling and then came the unwelcome sight of an overhang of rock barring their way.

'We'll have to swim underneath it,' Rufus said. 'Keep hold of your Glimper. Whatever you do, don't let go.'

Archie lay down on his stomach, and after a long intake of air, switched on his torch to act as a headlight. Then the Glimpers dived. Black icy water flowed past the beam of light guiding them around a bend in the rock that seemed to stretch on and on. Curiously, Archie felt no desire to breathe. His lung function was on hold. This gave his vision a dream-like quality, which was just as well, for as they emerged out of the bend they came face to face with a wall of Jellats. Oddly, they made no attempt to attack.

The only movement came from their tentacles, swaying in the strong swell of the water. Their mouths were opening and closing in a slow, helpless way, giving Archie a clear view of their razor-sharp teeth. Their glassy eyes watched him draw closer, but he could tell they were dying, their bodies ripped apart by Glimper claws. Even so, he still felt a mixture of trepidation and revulsion as he pushed the tentacles aside. He could feel their weight against his head and shoulders and their slimy touch on his face.

Archie caught a glimpse of Rufus, whose eyes were screwed up with the effort of trying not to breathe. He was pointing to something darting between the swaying tentacles.

Archie's finger was already pressed down hard on the green button by the time a set of beady eyes and sharp teeth burst through the tangle.

There was a brief frenzy of bubbling water and teeth grazing his hands and face as the torch beam turned the Jellat into a grey sludge. Archie kept his finger poised on the ready button, but there were no other surprise attacks and the Glimpers swam on through to the other side of the tentacle jungle. They emerged into clear water, dappled by daylight trickling down from above.

They had been underwater a long time; too long for Rufus, whose eyes were shut as if he had drifted off to sleep. Archie broke the surface first and gasped for air as he wiped the water from his goggles. Behind him he could see the mouth of the cave where earlier that morning Sid had fallen into the sea. Beside him was Rufus, lying unconscious on the back of the Glimper, and straight ahead and low in the sky was the unmistakable shape of a curse front closing in from the east.

Chapter Forty-five

Archie reached over and shook Rufus's motionless body. His eyes flicked open, his chest began to heave and he spluttered and coughed.

'I thought you were dead,' Archie told him.

'Not dead,' Rufus gasped. 'Just switched off. A very useful technique I picked up in Ecuador.' He wiped the water from his face, raised himself up on to one arm and sniffed the air. He looked around at the open sea. 'Did I miss anything?'

Archie pointed to a long flame-coloured spiral that was twisting and snaking down through the clouds. 'The eastern front is here.'

Rufus squinted and shook his head. 'I can't see what you're looking at.'

Archie pushed his goggles up on to his forehead and the spiral disappeared. In its place was the same grey and black cloud that Rufus was staring at. Archie pulled the goggles back down over his eyes and the spiral reappeared. He described what he was seeing to Rufus, who was trying to assess the situation. 'What's the angle?'

'Ninety degrees and moving fast towards Thomson's Beard,' Archie replied.

Rufus nodded. 'Keep pointing to the spiral. I want to check on its path.' After a second or two of watching Archie's moving finger, he confirmed what he suspected. 'The Glimpers are swimming in the wrong direction.'

Archie couldn't contain his frustration. 'Why would they do that? I thought they were here to help us.' He kicked his heels against the Glimper's shell. 'Go the other way!' he shouted. 'Turn round!' But they kept on swimming at a steady pace in the opposite direction.

Rufus remained calm. 'The Glimpers know what they're doing. Give them time.'

'We don't have time!' Archie told him. And then, as if things couldn't get any worse, the Glimpers stopped swimming altogether.

'They're useless, useless, useless . . .' Archie complained, but he was soon silenced by the unexpected sound of clanking metal. It grew steadily louder until there was one final ear-splitting crash that sounded as if scaffolding was collapsing and the sea around them flattened. A massive barnacled surface rose up out of the water and Archie and Rufus found themselves aboard a raft, constructed by Glimpers linking their legs together.

'Never underestimate a Glimper,' Rufus told him.

They dismounted from the crabs they had been riding and settled themselves on the raft. Rufus grabbed two lengths of washed-up Jellat tentacles and threaded them through the Glimpers' claws to make reins.

'Hold on tight,' he advised. 'It's going to be a bumpy ride.'

The raft swung round to the left and powered by a hundred sets of eight legs they began to surf the swell. It was littered with a layer of lifeless Jellat tentacles and rotting brown foam, but the Glimpers ploughed on, heading in the direction of Thomson's Beard.

Archie's eyes searched the sky. 'Miss Napier said two curse fronts would collide. One from the west and one from the east. Where's the other one?'

'Keep looking,' Rufus told him.

But Archie could see nothing other than a mass of grey and black cloud that joined an equally grey and black sea. There was no visible horizon, just wave after swollen wave. He felt his stomach rise and fall with the motion and he groaned as the raft was swept up on to the crest of a high wave. He was still scanning the sky when he caught sight of a mass of black shadows racing towards them, just above the surface of the water.

'It's here!' he shouted to Rufus. 'It looks like a spiderweb.'

'Those are curses waiting to be activated,' Rufus told

him. 'It must be high tide.'

Archie looked again at the flaming spiral. It was now so low in the sky that at times the waves blocked it completely from his view, but he could tell the two fronts were close to colliding and the raft was still some way off.

'Swim faster!' he shouted to the Glimpers, who appeared to be tiring.

'I think we may have a new and unexpected development,' he heard Rufus say.

Archie had been concentrating so hard on watching the two curse fronts, that he hadn't noticed the watery hands Rufus was referring to. They had emerged out of the sea and were holding on to the raft and slowing the Glimpers down.

'Water Devils,' Rufus explained. 'Their job is to keep us as far away as possible.' He pointed towards a long wave rising up in front of Thomson's Beard.

The wave didn't look like any of the others. This wave was made entirely from an army of powerful Water Devils, and as they advanced Archie realised he had seen their large watery skulls before, looking down on him through Mr Petrie's office window. He had also seen their long arms before, pouring from the broken pipe outside his classroom, and he'd heard their fingers drumming on the windowpanes at Windy Edge, the same fingers that were rocking the raft and trying to slow them down.

Archie pulled the torch from his belt and took aim.

'Don't!' Rufus told him. 'You could damage the Glimpers. We can't take that risk.'

The army of Water Devils continued to advance. They had no necks and their large skulls rested on powerful shoulders as broad as Ezekiel's boat. With each step forward their massive torsos emerged out of the sea, rising higher and higher until their huge bodies blocked out the sky and their strange expressionless faces were looking down on Rufus and Archie.

'I think the torch may need some help,' Rufus told him.

The Water Devils raised their thick arms and bowed to form a curved roof of water over the raft, sealing Archie and Rufus inside a long tunnel. It was eerily calm and unnaturally quiet.

Rufus pulled the magnifying glass out of Archie's rucksack and held it over the torch lens. 'Aim for the top of the tunnel,' he told Archie. 'When I give the word, fire in a circular motion.' Rufus helped Archie get into position and when they were ready he shouted, 'Fire!'

Archie pressed the button and the magnified light that poured from the torch was ten times more powerful and ten times hotter. As the light pierced the tunnel, the raft was thrown into a violent spin by seawater collapsing around them. Archie kept the white light aimed at the top of the wave but the torch was growing unbearably hot. Then, when Archie was sure his palms were about to melt, Rufus said, 'Switch off.'

They found themselves inside a mist that was falling as hot rain. All that was left of the Water Devils were wisps of skulls, arms and legs, drifting around the raft, turned to steam by the torch.

The Glimpers powered onwards through the treacherous waves, desperate to make up for lost time.

'We must be close to Thomson's Beard,' Rufus told Archie. 'Let's hope we're in time.'

Archie looked up at the sky as the last of the steam faded. A burning sensation had gripped the side of his neck and the sea turned the colour of blood.

'It's here,' he whispered.

'Where?' Rufus was asking.

But Archie was frozen. He was staring up into a boiling crater that was the mouth of the twisting coil.

The Glimpers stopped swimming and folded their claws in under the raft as the sea around them flattened. The web of curses rose up behind Archie, ready to cast itself over him like a fisherman's net.

'Give me your pebble,' Rufus was saying, but Archie was too terrified to move.

'I can't battle this,' he managed to whisper. 'It's too big.'

Archie felt Rufus take the pebble from his pocket and then he was being pulled up on to his feet. Rufus placed the torch into Archie's belt, folded his arms across his body and placed a pebble either side of his shoes. The arrows swung round to point east and west.

'You are now in the exact position to exterminate the two curse fronts,' Rufus was telling him. 'Keep your arms crossed. It'll double your resistance. Stay focused. You have the power to destroy them . . .'

The rest of Rufus's words were drowned out by the pounding in Archie's head. He wasn't aware of the raft moving any more, only of the power stemming from the spiral. It was pushing against his lungs like an invisible wall and the strength from the web of curses was pushing against his spine.

He couldn't breathe, and the roar of blood pounding in his head sounded like the engines of a powerful ship: a battleship with heavy guns and towering masts that had been rusting at the bottom of the sea for sixty years. He could see it now, its rusting hulk thrown up from the seabed by a ghostly time slip. It was powering towards him, throwing the sea aside in huge washes of water, its horn piercing his ears. 'It's not real, it's not real,' he kept telling himself, but as the bow hit the raft Archie shut his eyes. There was the creak and clank of metal twisting and then the SC56 finally struck.

Chapter Forty-six

Archie could hear strange animalistic howling and screeching. He could hear the hiss of water on fire, and ice cracking, and through the wail of the ship's horn there came the terrified cries of a thousand lost souls. He kept his eyes tightly shut, afraid of what he might see, but when he felt himself being raised up by the soles of his feet he instinctively opened them. What he saw made him shut his eyes again. He was balanced on the top of the battleship mast.

Far beneath him the sea was a foaming mass of broken waves and rising up out of this turbulence were the masts of other ghostly ships: schooners, ocean liners and sailing ships, draped in seaweed with ripped sails and screeching skeletal figures clinging to the rigging. One of those skeletal figures threw itself on to the mast Archie was standing upon and he could hear its bones rattle as it climbed up towards him.

This moment of terror had allowed Archie's

concentration to falter and he felt his force field weaken. He tried reaching for the dagger that was tucked into his belt, but his arms were paralysed by the invisible walls that were squeezing the life out of him. He had to find a way of driving them apart.

He tried to tap into the courage he had felt when he was back in the caves, destroying the Monstrum with the burning torch and turning the Water Devils to steam. Then he imagined he was channelling lightning strikes through the dagger tip – but none of it worked.

Then he thought of the herring gull crying, 'Save Rufus!' and his father holding the umbrella over his mother in the wheelchair, and George Ratteray saying, 'You Stringweeds are all the same.'

Archie's determination began to swell. Static sparks shot out from his body, the air around him crackled and the SC56 shuddered and moved.

As the force field grew stronger he found himself wrapped in a glowing shield of anti-curse power. He told himself that he would not let his defences falter again, regardless of what might confront him. Then he opened his eyes.

Before him, the swirling red inferno had taken the form of a serpent's face. It was performing the same swaying dance the serpents had carried out in front of the aeroplane as it prepared to connect with the web of curses. Archie held his nerve. When the serpent opened its mouth to reveal a set of Jellat teeth, and a skeletal hand reached up and grabbed his ankle, he knew it was another tactic to break his defences. He generated another anti-curse charge, the pressure against his body eased and he found he could move his arms.

But the physical effort of pushing back the walls of curse energy left him exhausted. The force field around his body dimmed and beyond it he could see the serpent's face contorted with boiling rage as it opened its mouth ready to strike.

The web of curses was closing in, too. Archie saw to his horror it was not made of shadows at all, but minuscule black creatures that looked human but for their bat wings and long tails that flicked above their heads.

He remained focused. 'Don't panic . . . make a sound judgment.'

He thought back to the vision he had seen through the telescope at I.C.E., of himself perched high above a turbulent sea with his arms crossed, just as they were now. He suddenly realised in this moment of clarity what the Mist of Knowledge had been telling him at the crossroads. If he were to succeed in exterminating the SC56, he must combine the power of the dagger and the torch.

He lowered his arms, making sure to keep them crossed, until the fingers of his right hand reached the dagger tucked in the left side of his belt. It shot up into his hand in a shower of static sparks and a rush of energy. He stretched his left hand towards the torch, and the second it was in his palm he felt power surge through his body. The combined effect created a stronger protective force field and Archie finally felt ready to face the SC56.

The serpent launched its attack and the web cast its net. Archie was caught inside a strange world of red and black turmoil. Long ashen faces covered in sores circled him. Screaming mouths, dripping blood, appeared out of nowhere, and bulging eyes hanging loose from their sockets stared out at him. He could see shape-shifting shadows that resembled the Monstrum, and diseased creatures with large gills and webbed feet filled the air with the smell of their rotting flesh. Among it all, millions of tiny winged creatures were crawling over his face.

Archie remained focused. He could barely breathe and he felt as if he was being squeezed out through the top of his head, but one by one the curses were turned to vapour.

He had no concept of time passing. It was only when the red and black turmoil began to fade and there were no more winged creatures trying to attack him that he knew the SC56 was weakening. When he caught a brief glimpse of grey sky, he knew the time slip was becoming unstable also.

The pressure against his spine and lungs eased and the burning pain in his arms and hands subsided. He could breathe, too.

The skeleton released its bony hand from his ankle and it leapt from the mast. The cries and wailing of the shadowy figures clinging to the rigging of the ghostly fleet gradually fell silent as the ships disappeared beneath the waves.

Archie was aware of being lowered too and when the rumbling of the battleship engines ceased, he looked down. He was standing on the raft and through the last traces of swirling vapour he could see the two pebbles either side of his feet, glowing bright green. He was finally back in the real world and someone was calling his name.

A tall thin figure was emerging through the haze.

'I *did* it, Rufus. I exterminated the SC56.'

But the figure that was now drifting towards him was not Rufus, but a thin column of dust and shadows. The face had only one eye and as the contorted mouth opened Archie raised the torch and dagger and turned Huigor to vapour.

Slowly the air cleared. There were no more serpents, webs or ghostly ships, just Rufus lying across the raft and the herring gull standing next to him. It threw back its head and gave a plaintive cry.

Archie uncrossed his arms and groaned. Every

muscle in his body throbbed and he dropped to his knees with exhaustion. He pulled the rucksack from his weary shoulders and was placing the torch and dagger safely inside it when Rufus suddenly lunged forward and pushed him flat on to the raft. Seconds later a smouldering boulder whistled past his ear.

'It's the tail end of the SC56,' Rufus told him as another rock landed close to the raft.

'Keep down,' Rufus warned as the bombardment continued. Archie grabbed the rucksack and had managed to loop it over one shoulder when the raft unexpectedly swung up on end to create a shield against the rock shower. He and Rufus were left clinging to the Glimpers' backs, their feet searching for footholds between the shells. Archie didn't know how much longer he could hold on. His hands were swollen and sore and his arms ached.

'Almost there,' Rufus reassured him. Then they heard a high-pitched whistle. 'Here comes the big one,' Rufus said. 'Brace yourself.'

A boulder, larger than any of the others, hurtled into the raft with a sickening force that threw them both into the sea. There was no time to swim clear before the raft came crashing down, knocking Archie unconscious. He sank helplessly through the water, his arms by his sides, oblivious to the rucksack slipping from his arm.

Chapter Forty-seven

The sea was thick with rotting Jellat bodies, but Archie didn't care. He just wanted to drift down through the rocking motion of the current. He didn't want to fight or think about anything any more, and he didn't care if he never took another breath, but a pair of bright green eyes was keeping him awake. He stretched his hand out to push them away and two green pebbles landed in his palm. 'Guard them with your life if necessary,' he heard Professor Himes say.

Archie wrapped his fingers around the pebbles and kicked his aching legs. He had allowed himself to drift a long way down through the sea and now he wanted to breathe.

As he struggled against the weight of the ocean, a hand gripped the neck of his jumper. His feet kicked something hard that made his legs buckle at the knees. Then he was being pushed upwards at a speed that made the water thunder in his ears. When his head at last broke the surface, his body heaved as his lungs pulled in the cold air.

Rufus was in the water beside him, holding on to the back of his jumper, but still Archie kept rising until he found himself sitting on the back of a Glimper that had pushed him to the surface.

He shook his head wearily and gasped, 'I lost the rucksack.' He opened his clenched hand. 'But I saved the pebbles.'

'And I got this!' Rufus replied, and he swung the rucksack out of the water and placed it beside Archie. His cheeks and nose were red and peeling from the SC56 but he managed a grateful smile. Then Rufus turned his attention to the capsized raft.

Four large crabs at the centre of the raft had taken the full impact of the boulder and their shells were cracked and broken. In order to reach them Rufus began to free the crabs on the outside of the raft first, but it was an impossible task. They were disorientated at being upside down and as soon as he freed one it would entangle itself again. Rufus was growing more and more concerned.

'If the Glimpers can't right themselves, they'll drown.'

'We can't let them die,' Archie told him. 'Not after they saved us.'

As he looked out over the swollen sea, he noticed a

single snowflake floating close by. Other snowflakes started to fall, where they melted on contact with the water, but the persistent snowflake continued to float towards him. Archie raised the goggles from his eyes and looked at it more closely.

What he saw made him look up into the sky.

A white cumulus cloud was drifting down and deep within it he saw telltale flashes of green light.

'Rufus! The Icegulls are here!'

Together they watched as a small flock of Icegulls emerged out of the snow flurry and landed gently on the raft. The Icegulls looked thinner than Archie remembered and their once bright green eyes were dull, too.

'They're weak,' Rufus explained. 'The regeneration process isn't complete. That's why there are so few of them.'

The birds quickly set to work, untangling the complex web of Glimper legs with their beaks until each crab had been released and pushed under water.

The whole operation was quietly efficient. The only sound came from the beat of the Icegulls' wings and the gentle knocking of busy beaks against the Glimpers' shells. In a matter of minutes the rescue mission was complete, apart from the four badly injured crabs at the centre of the raft, but that was swiftly taken care of. A team of small Glimpers emerged out of the sea and took up position beside the injured crabs. They began to secrete a sticky substance from their mouths which they used to repair and seal the injuries. When the operation was complete, they were gently pulled underwater, removing all trace of the raft.

Archie and Rufus were left to look out over the sea in the direction of Westervoe. The journey back home was going to be a long and uncomfortable ride.

But the Icegulls weren't finished. While the rest of the flock disappeared back inside the snow flurry, two birds remained. They puffed out their chests and spread their wings and expanded in size to accommodate a passenger. Then they took flight and circled as if to test their new size and, once satisfied of their strength, hovered beside Archie and Rufus, who climbed on to the warmth of the feathers.

The Icegulls didn't immediately head towards Westervoe. Instead they remained inside the snow flurry and hovered.

'What are they waiting for?' Archie asked.

His answer came with a rippling of the water and a full army of Glimpers rising up out of the sea like a rocky island. Thousands of claws were raised high before coming together with the metallic clash of heavy swords.

Three more times they gave this salute, each louder than the last, and the sound was still echoing in Archie's ears as the Glimpers sank back down into the sea. Not long after he heard the sound of distant marching, but this time it was the march of a victorious army heading home.

'Let's go,' Rufus said, and the Icegulls took flight.

They soared over the pod of whales they had met earlier, now heading back out to open sea, and not far beyond them was Ezekiel's boat.

'Never underestimate a Glimper!' Archie said as he pointed to a small platoon of crabs dragging the boat towards them.

They landed on the deck, and once Archie and Rufus were safely aboard the Icegulls shrank to the size of a seagull.

'They're weakening,' Rufus explained. 'They need to conserve their energy and return to their nesting grounds.'

The birds took flight and set off in the direction of Moss Rock, leaving behind two white feathers that Archie picked up and put in his rucksack.

Rufus, meantime, had fetched a waterproof jacket from the wheelhouse. Archie told him he didn't feel cold because he could still feel the effects of the force field, but Rufus insisted he wear it.

Archie was putting his arm into a sleeve when he revealed to Rufus, 'I saw Huigor after I exterminated the SC56. I blasted him with the torch. Do you think he's gone for good?'

Rufus looked out over the sea. 'Let's hope so, but until we have the four pebbles, anything is possible.' Then he smiled. 'Let's go home.'

He pulled up the anchor and started the engine. Archie took the binoculars from the wheelhouse and looked over the sea. There was nothing at all to suggest that Westervoe had just been saved from an SC56, except perhaps the layer of brownish froth and tentacles washed up on the shoreline.

The boat rounded the Point and as Westervoe came into sight the herring gull swooped overhead and landed on the deck. In its beak was a small Glimper that held something in its claw.

Archie stretched his hand out towards it and a tiny white shell fell lightly into his palm, but as he examined it more closely he saw it wasn't a shell at all, but Sid's missing tooth.

Chapter Forty-eight

No one took much notice of Rufus and Archie as they sailed back into harbour. A watery sun appeared from behind the clouds and for the first time in days the sea looked shiny and new. A bright rainbow straddled Westervoe and fresh air replaced the smell of decay. As if to confirm the sense of renewal, shoals of fish could be seen swimming in the harbour close to the pier.

The tide had already turned and with the sea level dropping, figures could be seen on the small piers jutting out into the harbour. They were busily mopping up the flood water, throwing huge clumps of washed-up seaweed back into the sea and surveying the damage. Rufus pointed to one figure in particular wearing a distinctive orange jacket and red baseball cap. Slaverin' Joe was fishing from the harbour wall and the speed at which he was casting and reeling in his line told them he was catching fish.

But Archie was more interested in looking up the hill, beyond the glistening wet roof tiles, to a column of smoke rising from the chimney at Windy Edge. Cecille and Jeffrey were home.

Once Rufus had secured the boat and stacked the creels at the back of the deck, they jumped ashore. The black Labrador was there to meet Rufus and it gave a single welcoming bark before accompanying them on their walk up the pier.

Their bedraggled appearance drew only a nod of acknowledgement from Slaverin' Joe, who was unhooking a salmon from his fishing line.

'Lucky you were out at sea and not here. Three big waves in succession washed right over the harbour. Damaged quite a few boats. Yes, you were very lucky.' He tossed the fish into a box, and then, as Archie and Rufus carried on walking towards the motorbike, he called out to them, 'Didn't happen to see any mermaids, did you?'

Archie shook his head. 'No mermaids.'

Archie and Rufus were approaching the motorbike when George came pedalling down the pier at breakneck speed. His fishing rod was in his hand and he wasn't scowling any more.

'There's hundreds of salmon in the harbour,' he said, as the bike came to a halt beside Archie. 'They broke loose from a fish farm.' He suddenly registered Archie's scorched cheeks and nose and his wet clothes, too. 'What happened? Don't say you fell in!' Then he noticed Rufus's wet clothes and his eyes filled with admiration. 'Did you dive in and save Archie?'

'Actually, Archie saved me!' Rufus told him.

George's mouth dropped as he watched Archie climb into the sidecar. Then he remembered the shoal of salmon and he set off on his bike with a big excited grin.

'Go home and get your fishing rod, Archie. I've got plenty of worms!'

Archie was eager to go home, but there was one thing he intended to do before heading up to Windy Edge.

Rufus drove the bike through the main street with the Labrador running alongside, until they reached Sid's house. Three small heads belonging to Sid's younger brothers popped up at the living room window to make faces at Archie while he stood ringing the doorbell.

Sid opened the door, and before he could ask any questions about Archie's bizarre appearance the tiny tooth was placed in his hand. He could only stare open-mouthed as Archie squelched towards the bike, climbed into the sidecar and waved goodbye in a flash of sparks.

When Archie and Rufus arrived back at Windy Edge they could tell Cecille and Jeffrey were unaware the

SC56 had already struck. Archie could hear Cecille in the kitchen humming along to a TV jingle and Jeffrey was piling more coal on to the roaring fire. He turned and smiled broadly when he saw Archie in the doorway.

'Told you we'd be back in good time.'

At the sound of voices, Cecille came hurrying out of the kitchen. 'There you are!' She opened her arms and hurried towards Archie with a big smile. 'I was getting worried about you two. The harbour was swamped during high tide. We saw the damage as we drove into Westervoe . . .'

She broke off as she registered Archie's scorched face and the big waterproof jacket and his soggy shoes. Then she noticed his ripped trousers and the deep scratch on his leg.

Jeffrey was looking at Rufus's similarly dishevelled appearance. 'Is this what I think it is?' he asked.

Rufus nodded.

Cecille was horrified. 'No . . . the SC56 isn't due until tonight!'

Rufus managed to stop his teeth chattering long enough to explain, 'You can't accurately predict curse movement any more than you can the weather.' And then he sneezed.

Cecille immediately began fussing over them, giving first aid for the scratch on Archie's leg, running baths and showers, making hot drinks and warming clean clothes on the radiators. Jeffrey kept telling her to sit down and he would see to it, but she was too wracked with guilt to listen.

'I knew we should have left Edinburgh earlier. I knew it.'

Jeffrey was feeling equally guilty. He was putting calamine lotion on Archie's red cheeks and peeling nose when he asked, 'How was it?'

Archie decided to keep his answer simple. 'It wasn't so bad. I just had to stand there and the two fronts sort of bounced off me.'

Jeffrey didn't look convinced, but before he could ask any more questions Archie excused himself by saying he was going up to his room to check on the artefacts. He didn't want to talk or think about the SC56 any more. He was just glad that it was all over.

The artefacts were laid out to dry on the radiator in his room. The Icegull feathers were clean and fluffy and the moisture clouding the watch face had started to clear. He noticed, too, that the planets inside the weatherscope had stopped vibrating and the glass was colourless again. Everything was back to normal. Well, almost everything.

He was shaking drops of water from the inside of the flute when Jeffrey knocked on the door and walked in. He was carrying a heavy blue holdall which he handed to Archie.

'What is it?' Archie asked.

'A tent. We're going camping up Ork Hill as soon as the weather improves.'

'Is it a promise?'

Jeffrey extended his hand. 'Shake on it!' But they both agreed not to shake after sparks flew between their fingers.

Cecille appeared in the doorway and asked, 'What's going on in here?'

'We're going on a camping expedition up Ork Hill,' Archie told her. 'Do you want to come?'

Archie didn't like the way she hesitated and said, 'Let's see how I'm feeling.' And he didn't like the way she was looking at Jeffrey, as though they were keeping a secret from him. An important one, too, he sensed by the way she was trying to change the subject by hanging his medals around his neck.

'I think you are far more deserving of these than me,' she said with a smile.

Archie wasn't prepared to let her change the subject.

'I thought you were feeling better.'

Jeffrey turned serious. 'A lot of things have happened since December. Breaking the Stringweed curse changed our lives. With some things you can see the difference. My jogging, for example . . .' He hesitated. 'But it's the things you can't see that change your life the most.'

None of this was making any sense to Archie. 'There's something wrong, isn't there?'

Cecille shook her head and smiled. 'What your father is trying to say is you're going to be a brother, Archie. We're having a baby.'

Archie looked horrified. 'A baby!'

'Not till October!' Jeffrey added. 'Gives us all time to get used to the idea.'

He put an arm around Cecille and they stood smiling at Archie, waiting for his reaction. He could tell they were nervous so he managed a smile and said, 'Great.' In fact he wasn't sure it was 'great' at all. It would need a great deal more thought but right then all he wanted to do was rest.

After a cheese sandwich and a bowl of soup Archie stretched out on the sofa. He must have dropped off to sleep because the next thing he knew it was dark outside and Rufus was showing Professor Himes into the living room.

'Archie!' said the Professor, and he could hardly contain his jubilation as he shook Archie's hand. 'Congratulations! A job well done. Thank you for saving the people of Westervoe from what could have been a very nasty incident indeed. I have already given my sincerest thanks to Rufus, who has briefed me on all that happened today.'

Miss Napier followed the Professor into the room.

She sounded quite unlike herself because for the first time in nearly two weeks her nasal passages were clear. Her voice was light and easy as she commended his bravery.

'A wonderfully courageous job. Congratulations to you and Rufus on a splendid team effort. Marvellous, marvellous!'

Archie was so embarrassed by her enthusiastic praise that he decided to change the subject.

'I can see the colour of my eyes in the bucket of Icegull breath in my room,' he told her. 'Would you like to see it?'

While Cecille and Jeffrey looked at one another and said, '*Icegull breath?*' Miss Napier gasped with excitement.

'I most certainly would like to see it! But firstly, I would like to make a telephone call,' and she dashed out into the hall.

'She's calling I.C.E.,' the Professor explained.

They could hear Miss Napier on the phone saying, 'Yes! Icegull breath! In a bucket. In his room! Isn't that just absolutely marvellous!' Miss Napier called Archie to the phone. 'Quickly! The team has something to say to you.'

He put his ear to the phone and a chorus of voices sang 'For he's a jolly good fellow' three times, followed by three 'Hip! Hip! Hoorays!'

Archie was still smiling when Miss Napier took charge and finished her call. Then she turned to him and said, 'Now, Archie. May I please take a look at this bucket of Icegull breath?'

They climbed the stairs to the attic and Miss Napier leaned over the bucket and peered into it. After a moment or two she raised the pair of glasses she kept on a chain around her neck and placed them on top of the pair she was already wearing.

'Beautiful, beautiful,' she muttered as she stared into the bucket. When she finally stood up, Archie could see huge magnified tears in the corners of her eyes. 'It's a long, long time since I've seen Icegull breath of such purity.'

'You know everything about curses, don't you, Miss Napier?'

'Oh no! Not everything. There is always something new to learn. That is the nature of our work.'

She looked at the bucket again and sighed. 'All I need now are a few Icegull feathers. Mine are becoming rather worn out.'

Archie picked up to the two feathers drying on the radiator and handed them to her.

Miss Napier shook her head in amazement. 'You really are an extraordinary boy, Archie. I expect great things of you in the future.'

She stroked one of the feathers and her expression

changed, as though the feather was telling her something. She walked over to the window and using all her strength pulled up the swollen frame and stuck her head out into the night.

'Come and see this,' Archie heard her say.

Together they looked up through the tree branches at green flickering light covering the sky and in the distance a white cumulus cloud.

Miss Napier couldn't contain her excitement and her eyes seemed to sparkle with the reflected green glow.

'Regenerated Icegulls,' she gasped. 'Isn't that a wonderful sight?' And she breathed in the night air without a hint of nasal congestion.

'Where are the Icegulls going?' Archie asked.

'They are going to where they are needed,' was all Miss Napier would say. She removed both pairs of glasses and, although her eyes had returned to their usual size, they held a power that could look deep inside him. 'It's time you got some rest and we were on our way back to I.C.E.'

Jeffrey was summoned to carry the bucket of Icegull breath downstairs. Rufus sealed it with cellophane to stop spillages and then it was loaded into the car. Miss Napier held the bucket steady between her knees and then she and the Professor waved goodbye and drove off in a cloud of exhaust fumes.

When Archie finally went back upstairs to bed, the

green glow was still there in the sky. He lay watching the cumulus cloud drift across the skylight while listening to the night-time sounds of the house.

Gradually the talking turned to whispers; he heard the tiptoe of footsteps on the stairs and finally the click of light switches turning the house to darkness. All that was left was the chime of the grandfather clock.

He closed his eyes, ready to dream of flying away with a flock of Icegulls, but it was a lone herring gull he saw, bobbing up and down upon a calm sea. It was looking at him with a steady gaze that invited him to follow, and when its eyes turned a fluorescent green and Archie heard a voice deep inside his head say, 'He who has vision sees beyond the horizon,' he smiled.

The ocean stretched far into his dream, but tonight it held no fear, and he snuggled down into his blue quilt, found a gentle wave all of his own, and drifted off to sleep.